The YOUNGISH MARRIEDS

A BETWEEN HEAVEN AND HELL NOVEL

I0587835

L A MICHAELS

LML BOOKS

Cover Design by: Polyarts36

Front and back cover images by: Luviiilove

Edited and proofed by Sandra Watts

OTHER BOOKS BY L A MICHAELS

BETWEEN HEAVEN AND HELL

THE INNOCENT YEARS

I LOVE YOU, I HATE YOU, I MISS YOU

NOVELLAS

OUR PRIVATE WORLD APART

For Luviiilove.

An artist and visionary. Thank you for helping create the Between Heaven and Hell universe.

Pastiche:

An artistic work in a style that imitates that of another work, artist, or period.

Soap Opera:

An ongoing drama serial on television or radio, featuring the lives of many characters and their emotional relationships.

From the flames of a fire to the blue skies above, we are all just somewhere Between Heaven and Hell...

NIAL JANUARY 2019

"*Paging Dr. Nial Fitzpatrick... Paging Dr. Nial Fitzpatrick to the third-floor nurses' station,*" said a nurse who clearly had something against Nial. He wasn't entirely sure why. It wasn't as if he had slept with her and not called back. That said, lately, he could not remember much. It was one quickie after another. Nial had been fucking women like a jackrabbit as of late. It all started after his instant-fiancé had left him back in October. She had a great wrack and a great ass, but not much else going for her. It all went to hell when his estranged daughter showed up in Switzerland out of nowhere for a visit.

Nial had not seen Laura in years, and Laura was pissed to find out that Nial had been sleeping with a woman only six months older. The blonde doctor himself had to admit that once it was spelled out, he too grew disturbed, and that was the end of that relationship. His last long-term relationship had been with his mistress that he had also planned to marry. She had been cheating on him with an intern half his age named Austin Martin.

Nial may or may not have had him killed by a lifelong friend of the family and alleged crime boss Anthony Costa's right-hand man. Nial had never been caught, but when his older sister Margot found out, he was kicked out of the country. She wasn't pissed off that he had offed someone. She had done it herself with her own hands once or twice. It was more or less that he had used one of their free kills on a waste of space.

Since he and the blonde bimbo had parted ways, he had moved back stateside but had been working at a hospital in Illinois somewhere in-between Springfield and Oakdale, not too far from Bay City. He had been offered jobs in upstate New York and Pennsylvania, but he liked being closer to Michigan, where he had grown up. It also gave him a slight thrill that he was so close to home, but his bitch of a sister and whore of an ex-wife Vivica were none the wiser of just how close he really was.

The middle-aged male doctor walked towards the desk. Nial wore designer clothes even at work. There was no such thing as owning second best in his mind. He still had his blonde hair and few wrinkles, which he was pleased about, as his striking blue eyes were essential to sealing the deal on his many flings. He worked out twice a day for two hours at a time. He had no plans to ever be out of shape.

"What is it?" he asked the nurse, who clearly had an

attitude with him.

"Dr. Fitzpatrick, you have a guest who insists on you coming to him as opposed to waiting in your office," the nurse explained.

If he had to guess, this meant that Margot had discovered where he was and was pissed. He knew sure as hell that Vivica, who was engaged, would not be coming to visit him. Nial turned around and took a large gulp... Anthony Costa.

Anthony Costa was your classic Italian gangster. Well-dressed but made it clear that they were up to no good. Anthony had been able to avoid jail over the years because of an excellent legal team. His late uncle had been best friends with Nial's parents in their young adulthood, and Anthony was sent to live with them from New York after his own parents were *tragically* murdered by the police.

He and Nial had spent their summers together while he was home from his boarding school. They got along famously, aside from a few instances over the years. It didn't scare Nial any less than the Italian man who was standing here.

He was unsure if he had mentioned to Anthony that he was living in Illinois. The doctor knew he had mentioned moving back stateside, but that was about it. "Anthony, what brings you by?" Nial said with a genuine smile.

The mob king smiled, "I just thought maybe we could catch up on a few things."

"Oh well, of course. Anything for an old friend," Nial

said as he held back a gulp. Anthony was such a powerful man, even just in his voice. The blonde doctor wasn't even sure why he was so afraid of him. He has been friends with him for so long. It was just whenever Anthony wanted anything, it never ended well for him or the rest of the Fitzpatrick family. His own son Brad was Preston Costa for months on end when he was a baby because of the Costa family drama.

"You know my son is dating your nephew," Anthony explained. "At least that is what I've heard. Preston won't take the boy home when he knows we are around."

This was a piece of information that Nial was unsure what to do with. "You are telling me that Preston is dating Perry?" he asked in shock. Perry was close to thirty, and Preston was still in high school. He also had no idea either of them was gay. He honestly couldn't give a damn if two people were gay. It just meant more women for him.

Anthony rolled his eyes, "No, Harry... I mean, technically, he isn't your nephew anymore, but technicalities are technicalities," the slick backed haired man explained.

Harry, the boy who used to hide behind Vivica when *The Muppets* were on TV, was dating a boy like Preston? He had heard of Preston's reputation, and it was not much better than Anthony's. Then again, he should not have judged him based on his father. None of his children were anything like him. "Well, good for them, I suppose. I mean, do you really want your son dating a Knight, though?"

There was silence for a minute, "Not really. That Cliff

is a piece of work. Though you know that better than anyone."

Lord did Nial know about how big a piece of work Cliff was. He remembered all three of his marriages to Vivica very well. She was head over heels in love with Cliff. It did not matter that he was married to her sister and that he chose this. It wasn't like he was tricked into being with Tiffany. Nial had to admit he wasn't that fond of Tiffany himself. She was overly confident and always felt like the real gold digger out of the two Weston sisters. Yet, time labeled Vivica The Whore from Beverly Hills, and Tiffany was the perfect little doctor... If only people had the same front window to that whole ordeal back in the '90s as he had.

VIVICA— April 1990

"Mother! Mother! Can you not hear me?" screamed the red-haired vixen as she descended from the staircase of the Weston-Brash family home. It wasn't as if it was a long flight of stairs, but it did not change the fact that her mother, Gale Brash, refused to answer her.

Gale walked into the living room from the kitchen. She was already dressed in a sundress. They had been invited to their in-laws, the Fitzpatrick's, for dinner that night. It was the first night that Nadia and Brandon's son Nial would be back from school, and Gale had accepted the offer to spend the evening with them.

It had been a tough couple of years with the death of Gale's husband, DJ Brash, who had been the half-brother of Nadia. Nadia and Gale managed to overcome their issues with one another and had become very close since DJ's passing. In that time, Gale had gone to work for *The Fitzpatrick Group,* which the Fitzpatrick family, of course, owned. She didn't really have to work because DJ's life insurance had been so high. However, Gale enjoyed being close to his family. It kept him alive for her.

"Vivica, what on earth did you need that you felt the need to scream loud enough Mrs. Templeton can hear from her cellar?" the mother asked her daughter.

Vivica sighed. Her mother would never learn. "I have nothing to wear, so I guess that means I can't go," Vivica explained.

The mother rolled her eyes, "I don't really think they care what you wear so long as you put in some form of effort. You haven't seen your cousin in a few years, thanks to all the traveling that you have been doing."

Vivica was currently one of the most prominent faces in the fashion modeling world. It had been that way for the past few years since Vivica took an offer back in high school to do a summer of modeling in New York. It only got bigger for her to the point where she successfully argued against going to college.

As the two continued to argue, the front door opened. In walked a raven-haired girl wearing a plaid dress with worker boots on. "Hi, mom!" Tiffany said as she closed the door behind her. She looked at her younger sister and gently nodded.

"Oh no! She better not be coming with us!" Vivica screamed at Gale.

Gale sighed, "No, Vivica, your sister is not going to be coming with us. She is just borrowing a cookbook from me."

The tone of voice that her mother took honestly offended her. Gale had insisted on Vivica coming with her to Grosse Pointe when she divorced her father. She was forced to live here for years while Tiffany got to stay in Beverly Hills, California. It was not fair then, and it still was not fair now. Tiffany had pretty much been absent from their lives, minus a few random phone calls every so often. Then she decided to transfer to college here randomly, and from there everything went downhill.

"Mother, I would appreciate it if you didn't allow the woman who stole my fiancé into our house," Vivica crossed her arms.

Tiffany scoffed, "I did not steal Cliff! You two were broken up, and I didn't even know you had dated him until months into our relationship," Tiffany explained.

Didn't know about their relationship? Gale had forced Vivica to send pictures to her father and Tiffany her entire life. Vivica had known Cliff since she moved to town and had been best friends with him up until they were sixteen. That is when they had started to date.

They were engaged when Vivica got the opportunity of a lifetime to go to Australia for six months to be a muse to an up-and-coming designer. Cliff had not been happy about it, but Vivica was not going to let her career go downhill that early on. She loved Cliff with all her heart, but they left on bad terms. They, however, never made any verbal indication to one another that they had broken up.

Tiffany had transferred to the same college that Cliff had been attending and just happened to meet on campus, where they happened to get drunk one night and get married. Vivica returned home to find them living together.

"Get the cookbook and leave," Vivica headed towards the staircase.

The older Weston sister took a deep breath, "Wait, Vivica... Look, Phyllis was wondering if you would like to come over sometime. She misses you greatly," Tiffany told her.

Phyllis was Cliff's younger half-sister. She was only eight years old. She and Vivica had a sisterly bond, and she understood Phyllis was not fond of Tiffany. The only person in the Knight household aside from the clearly brainwashed Cliff that seemed to like Tiffany was the head of the family, Rodrick. Well, head of the family in his own mind. Rodrick's mother, Delia, still reigned as Queen of the family with an iron fist.

Vivica turned back around, "Tell her I've been thinking about her but that I'm too busy. Honestly, I do not care what you tell her, but I have no desire to go to North Pointe anytime soon." Vivica turned back around and stormed up the staircase. She hated her sister with a passion. It was not that she did not understand where her mother was coming from. Tiffany was her daughter as well, but she should have known better than to let Tiffany into this house while she was still home. In Vivica's humble opinion, this house was Gale and Vivica's and no one else's since DJ had passed on.

DJ was the only father figure she had ever had, and she knew damn well that DJ would have sided with her, even if only out of fear.

She walked into her room and slammed the door. She went over to her vanity and opened the drawer. There was a picture of her and Cliff only a year or so ago. They were so happy. They had been engaged right outside of high school and had made plans even before they had officially gotten together as teenagers for what the future would hold. It was all out the door now, though. Vivica would never forgive Cliff Knight. Never.

CLIFF – JANUARY 2019

The wedding was two weeks away. After months of preparation, it was finally here after years of going back and forth as to whether they belonged to one another. Cliff Knight the Second was finally going to marry his Weston. Vivica Weston- Fitzpatrick- Knight- Fitzpatrick-Fitzpatrick would soon forever be known as just Vivica Knight. To be specific, Mrs. Cliff Knight because her only legal marriage to a Knight had been to his cousin. They had technically been married for a long time, but it turned out that his now ex-wife Tiffany was alive and well. He was forever grateful for this, but the reality is that Tiffany was not his soulmate. They were meant to have children together, but that was about it.

Vivica was the only woman that Cliff ever loved. It took years of guilt for him to accept this piece of information and he hated saying it out loud or even to himself, but the circumstances behind his marriage to Tiffany had been complicated.

The Knight CEO walked into the drawing-room at North Pointe. North Pointe was the Knights' ancestral family mansion that owned the *Knight Motor Company,* which was second in the big four US-manufactured auto industry. It had slipped in only a few months due to some money situations that Cliff and his daughter Hannah had been trying to sort. The Drawing Room was currently wedding central. In Cliff's mind, this was going to be the wedding of the century based on just how big of an ordeal it was turning into. Originally, they had planned a big wedding, then only a few months ago in September, they had decided on a quick wedding.

Cliff's children Hannah and Harry and Vivica's son Brad along with Vivica's maid Holly had all flat out refused a quick wedding. They were the ones who wanted this big production. Though he suspected that Vivica also wanted it and only said she wanted something simple to appease him.

On the other hand, Cliff wanted nothing more than to please Vivica in any way that he could. This would be the most important day to them, next to all their children's births, which of course did not compare in the slightest.

However, based on this wedding's cost and size, their wedding album was sure to rival all five of their children's baby books in terms of size. That was more due to the insistence of the photographer who was giving them a discount to take the photos in the first place.

"There you are!" Holly O'Dell screamed. Holly was

Vivica's maid for the last six years. She had only recently transitioned into being on the North Pointe staff as a maid. Cliff had to make it a point to explain to the butler and head maid that while Holly had the title of a maid, she was essentially there because she and Vivica had an unhealthy bond towards one another. Cliff honestly did not mind Holly, but Holly's husband wasn't exactly fond of the amount of time Holly spent with Vivica instead of their family, which Cliff could understand to some degree.

"I have to get your confirmation on the seating chart. Bridget Madwell and her daughter Amanda will be in attendance. Bridget is expected to be a bridesmaid. So, she will be at the bridesmaid table along with Hannah, Lucy, and a Mrs. Brianna Belle. However, do we place Amanda with Langley? This gets tricky because Langley is technically Brad's plus one. If we are going to let Preston sit with Harry, then Langley will want to insist upon sitting with Brad even if Vivica doesn't want Lauderdale as she put it sitting anywhere near her son. I also still have no confirmation from Laura."

This was all too much for Cliff to process before leaving for work for the day. "Holly, please tell me you didn't just say Bridget Madwell was going to be at this wedding?"

The maid crossed her arms, "I just told you that Bridget Madwell is going to be a bridesmaid. Did you not hear me?"

Before he could say anything further, Vivica walked into the room. She had a bright smile on her face. Cliff looked at her.

"Bridget Madwell was invited to this wedding?"

The red-haired Vixen gulped on a sip of her coffee.

"I thought we had talked about this already..." Vivica said awkwardly.

"You know I can't stand Bridget Madwell!" Cliff practically screamed. He took a deep breath, "Sorry, it's just given the circumstances that prolonged this wedding, do you really think it is appropriate for her to be there?"

Bridget Maxwell, who is the owner and CEO of *The Madwell Modeling Agency,* had been Vivica's bad influence in the late '80s into the mid-'90s. They had temporarily parted ways when they both got pregnant around the same time. Cliff could not stand Bridget. It was only last year that Bridget had arranged for Vivica to revive her career temporarily on two separate occasions, which found Vivica hopping around the world as she avoided dealing with issues involving her and Cliff.

Vivica smiled, "Look, I know you and Bridget don't get along, but I don't get along with any of your old basketball friends that are coming or about half the people from Knight that you have insisted upon inviting. Bridget will be in some photos, and that will be the end of it. I doubt she will want to spend much time here. That said, I have other reasons for bringing her and Amanda to Grosse Pointe."

Vivica looked at Holly's seating chart. "Holly, why isn't Amanda at the same table as Brad? Lysistrata can sit with the band and photographer."

It took Cliff only a minute to realize what was going on, at least slightly. "Vivica, you can't trick your son into falling for

Bridget's daughter."

"Do you really think I would do a thing like that?" Vivica asked out loud.

Neither Cliff nor Holly answered. They both knew that Vivica had a disturbing hatred for Langley and Brad's relationship. They had briefly separated back in September but had been going strong since then. Vivica couldn't stand it. Cliff was honestly not sure if Vivica really could not remember Langley's name or not, but for some reason, every time, she said it completely wrong.

Cliff had to get to work, and at the end of the day, dealing with Bridget Madwell for a few days wasn't going to be the end of the world.

"Look, I don't care where anyone sits so long as I'm next to you the entire day. I must get to work. I have a meeting with Hannah, and she already left for the morning," He kissed Vivica on the lips quickly before running out the front door.

VIVICA – JANUARY 2019

"Do you think it was a mistake inviting Bridget?" Vivica asked Holly, her maid and best friend in the world. Holly looked at her for a solid second, "Is this really the ideal time to separate Brad and Langley?"

Probably not, but it was her wedding. It would be the perfect wedding gift. "Look, it isn't my fault that my son and nephew both are dating people that are completely wrong for one another," Vivica explained to Holly.

She could not stand the fact that her nephew Harry was dating the son of Anthony Costa and Jackie Carson-Costa. Anthony being a mob boss was hard enough. It was dealing with Jackie that drove Vivica up a wall. That woman hated other women. She had no female friends, maybe minus a slight liking towards Vivica's ex-sister-in-law Margot Fitzpatrick.

Considering that Vivica and Margot had hated one another since Vivica's late mother married her late stepfather DJ, who happened to be Margot's half-uncle, they were not exactly on great terms. However, their hatred had nothing to do with family relations, at least not at first. No, their hatred had to do with the fact that Vivica stole the metaphorical crown of Queen of Grosse Pointe from her. Vivica had been the reigning princess when she stole the crown. Margot was probably the shortest reining metaphorical Queen after the very long run of Boots Sinclair; a personal friend of Vivica's who, of course, would attend the wedding. Unfortunately, though, Vivica also had to extend an invitation to Margot. Mostly because of Brad and because her ex-business partner, who would be a bride's maid at the wedding, Lucy Kingsley was dating Margot's son Perry. At least Nial was out of the country as far as she knew.

It was as if fate was playing games. As Vivica briefly thought about Nial, she received a text message. She showed Holly in silence, "This cannot be happening right now."

Holly made a fist, "Why on earth is your ex-husband moving back to Grosse Pointe only two weeks before your wedding? Vivica, you need to avoid him like the plague."

If she were honest with herself, it offended Vivica greatly that Holly thought she was planning on meeting up with Nial intentionally. Vivica's relationship with Nial had always been one of lust and convenience. It was something that she felt both she and Nial agreed on. The first time they got married, Nial was looking to piss off his parents, and she was looking to piss off Cliff.

The second time they had married was to collect a large sum of money willed to the two of them. The third time they had married, it was out of a momentary lapse of sanity, which lasted a whole five years and ended with Nial officially announcing that he had been cheating on her. How many times was still up in the air, but at least once with a woman that had possibly faked a pregnancy or something. Vivica was not entirely sure and honestly didn't care. If she had not been married to Nial at the time, she probably would have pitied the girl for being pregnant with Nial's child.

As a doctor, Nial was great. As a father, he lacked a lot of common sense. Because of the blonde doctor, their son Brad was sent off to the same boarding school that he had gone to during his own childhood. Vivica had no idea what possessed him to think that was a good idea. She only went along with it at first because Nial had tricked Brad into thinking it was a good idea.

Their daughter had not spoken to them in years. Vivica honestly did not know if this was her fault, his fault, or both. She seldom ever heard from Laura. In her opinion, it was sad how little of a relationship she had with her own daughter, especially in comparison to the one she had with her mother growing up. It wasn't as if Vivica and Gale had ever been all that close. However, they spent practically every day together in some way, shape, or form until she started to model on a more national and then global level.

"We will just have to do our best to ignore it. Nial will taunt Cliff and I, but he cares too much about Brad's opinion to drive us up a wall. Honestly, I don't understand the love and admiration the Fitzpatrick's get. Having been one even before my marriage, I can tell you they are some of the most obnoxious people I've ever had the pleasure of dealing with." Vivica could think of one Fitzpatrick in general that fit this personality.

MARGOT- JANUARY 2019

Margot hated winter. Not as much as she hated autumn but definitely not as much as she hated spring. Though she also wasn't very fond of summer. It was all about that small in-between sometime in late March where it was the perfect temperature. It did not last exceptionally long, and the rest of the year, she was a miserable mess. Her birthday wasn't even in March. So, essentially, she was miserable even on her birthday.

A lot of people called her a piece of work because of this. It didn't bother Margot, who was the CEO of *The Fitzpatrick Group,* her family's company, which had been formed shortly before her birth and had come out of *Fitzpatrick Steel,* which was still a large part of the company, and they still owned and operated it.

It was the meeting of her book club. Or well, Mrs. Templeton's book club. Absolutely horrible woman, but she ran the damn best book club in town, the best wine, the best titles, and the best gossip.

The only downside was having to deal with Mrs. Templeton. Margot and those invited were all in agreement on the subject. She noticed that her whore of an ex-sister-in-law Vivica, was nowhere to be seen during this meeting. Her new employee Lucy Kingsley however, was. Lucy had also just started dating her son Perry. Margot didn't hold it against Lucy that she would date such a wishy-washy individual. While some people might have blamed her for how Perry turned out, she felt it was his own fault or maybe because of his loser father. It was not her fault, though, and she was prepared to fight anyone who disagreed.

The redhead looked at Lucy. Lucy was pretty, but she was too good-natured for anyone to really find her sexy. Margot had been sexy once. It was a long time ago, though. She couldn't give a damn at this point in life. It was all about making money and collecting ponies. She had the state's largest collection of plastic pony figures. It wasn't something that she publicly bragged about, but it was one of the few things in the world that gave her joy.

"You will enjoy this meeting. It's the best place to get the local gossip," she explained to Lucy.

"I've heard a lot about it over the past few years from Vivica," Lucy admitted.

The CEO rolled her eyes, "Yes, you heard a lot from Vivica. She had no power to score you an invite, though, as I did. That is one of the billions of differences between Vivica and I."

Originally, Lucy wanted to come work for her back when she first came to town. Margot didn't feel she was quite ready, though. Then the next thing she knew, she had taken on an assistant job working for Vivica, who has just started a party planning company with Margot's brother Nial's money. It was not even that she needed the money or job herself. She made money through modeling and her first two divorces from Nial. She also had stock within the Fitzpatrick Group from each of her divorces.

Lucy watched as their host for the evening, Mrs. Templeton, walked around the room, nodding at everyone. She stopped at Lucy and Margot. She looked directly at Lucy,

"You're the one who spends all your time with that red-haired whore?"

There was no proper way to respond to this, so Lucy just nodded, and Mrs. Templeton walked away. She turned to Margot, "So, when do we discuss the actual book?"

"No one talks about the book at a book club. Have you ever been to a book club before?" Margot asked her.

Not since she was in middle school. The eldest Kingsley child was regretting not listening to Perry's advice and declining the invitation. She had spent the time reading the lousy book when she could have been doing anything else, such as dealing with her father and lawyer threatening different things on her.

Ever since her father got out of jail, he had been begging her to speak on his behalf at his trial. She had no interest in returning to that lifestyle, though, unlike her sister Langley who was finally starting to properly adjust to small-town living.

LANGLEY — JANUARY 2019

A year ago, Langley Kingsley had been living in Manhattan attending an elite day school. She had many people that she would hang out with after school and on weekends. They were equally as beautiful and smart as she was, but she really was not their friends at the end of the day. None of them had really been friends with one another. They all just partied together, slept with one another, and switched partners regularly. Then one day, she would be expected to go to an Ivy and be married by twenty-five and a child by thirty.

Now she lived in Grosse Pointe and had a real friend group. She spent her weekends listening to the trials and tribulations of her friends' lives and going to the mall. Her best friend and first friend in Michigan happened to be Harry Knight. The son of the CEO of the Knight Motor Company. Her boyfriend was Brad Fitzpatrick, son of a world-renowned doctor and fashion model whose family happened to be owners of the Uber wealthy Fitzpatrick Group.

Harry's boyfriend was none other than Preston Costa. The son of alleged crime boss Anthony Costa and his art gallery owning wife Jackie Carson Costa. She and Preston had the same personality with a different set of genitalia. The Weston blooded cousins Harry and Brad were both saving themselves for marriage, which meant that Langley and Preston were currently not getting laid. Something they both had learned to accept in secret.

"Harry Knight, I am not going to wear that awful pink dress..." Langley rolled her eyes at her best friend.

The Knight boy sighed, "You wanted me to help you with an appropriate outfit to wear for the engagement party."

She wanted him to help her find an outfit so she could tell Brad that Harry had given input. She didn't want him to find the ugliest dress possible in hopes that Brad would think she was an expecting mother living in Clinton Township. "We need to find a different dress," Langley explained.

The engagement party for Cliff Knight and Vivica, well, she wasn't entirely sure what the last name she was going by at the moment. In other words, Harry's father and Brad's mother. It was already obvious that Vivica was not a fan of Langley. She wasn't even entirely sure that Vivica knew what her name was. Brad and Harry both insisted otherwise, but the red-haired model tended to call her every word that started with L but her own name.

"I need to look appropriate in Vivica and Brad's eyes, which is difficult considering how damn different the mother and son are..."

Brad had grown up surrounded by the idea that his parents were not the ideal role models that they were supposed to be. In his mind, they should have been more in tune with that of a 1950's sitcom instead of that of a 1980's prime time soap opera.

Vivica was a semi-retired supermodel, and Nial was a skirt-chasing doctor. They had married one another three times over. Their eldest child, Laura, had not spoken to any of them regularly since she turned eighteen.

Brad had an older half-brother from Nial as well that he seldom spoke about. Harry was the closest thing to a sibling that he had in his life. His father decided that Brad needed to go off to boarding school at one point, though much like him.

The difference was that Brad was not his father at all, and Brad strived and prided himself on being the complete opposite. The virgin until marriage son had morals and lived a very conservative life. Though not conservative against human rights as he was, of course, Harry's biggest supporter. That did not mean he supported Harry's relationship with Preston Costa, though.

"Do you own any long sleeve dresses?" Harry asked her.

The blonde looked at him like he was an idiot, "Do I need to wear gloves too? I better go buy a nun's outfit. For crying out loud, I could wear that, and I'd still be considered shutting it up for Brad in his and his mother's mind," she screamed into a pillow.

Harry smiled at Langley, "I think you will be fine so long as you dress appropriately. I mean, do you honestly think that aunt Vivica is going to have time to pay attention to you? She will be dealing with the press and all her random friends that show up."

She supposed that he was right. She got a text from Brad. He was in his basketball uniform. She loved a man in a basketball uniform. There was just something so sexy about it. There was something she noticed, though, right away. He had a slight bulge in his shorts. She quickly zoomed in and then quickly put her phone down. Langley did not need this temptation. It was a sick tease from some higher power. She wished that Brad's parents had not been the biggest sluts in town so that Brad would just fuck her already.

MARGOT – APRIL 1990

The elder Fitzpatrick child walked into her family home, pushing a stroller in front of her. Her elder son, Joshua, was on her side. He was twelve and home from boarding school. She slammed the door behind her. It opened right after, with her husband Paul Fields walking in behind her.

Paul was an average looking man that Margot herself had only married at first to merge his company into The Fitzpatrick Group. Then she ended up pregnant and started to fall for him. He was just average in every sense of the word. They made better friends than a husband and wife, but Margot was not about to get divorced again. At least he brought her Perry, the baby in the stroller. At least, that is what she kept telling herself.

Nadia Fitzpatrick, Margot's mother, walked into the

foyer from the kitchen. "Well, hello Margot," she said with a fake happy tone.

Margot was no idiot, her mother and her had never gotten along ever. She was only civil because of Joshua and newly born Perry. Possibly even Paul. It was sad that her own mother liked Paul more than her. It did not bother Margot, though.

"Where are your maids and the damn butler? We were knocking and ringing the bell for a good five minutes," Margot screamed at her mother.

"It's Easter, dear. We don't tend to have the staff work on Easter. Regardless, you know we keep the door open," Nadia explained to her, now rubbing her forehead.

The daughter rolled her eyes at her mother, "Mother, you can't leave the damn door unlocked anymore. There are serial killers and rapists on every corner." She handed the baby bag to Paul, "And for crying out loud, my staff is at our house today."

The Spanish mother and grandmother nodded her head,

"Yes, well, that is your choice. How is Rochester Hills, by the way?"

Such a catty way to change the subject. How did she think Rochester Hills was going? "It's wonderful. I love the Millionaire Mile. It makes sure that everyone knows what I am and what I embrace," Margot explained.

Margot walked towards the staircase and touched the railing. "Is Nial upstairs?"

Nadia sighed, "Yes." She cleared her throat and called up the stairs, "Nial! Young man get down here. Your sister is here."

It took about a minute, of which time they were all in silence for Nial to walk down the stairs. He had grown so fast. The last time she had seen him, Margot could have sworn he was only a freshman in high school, and yet he was now a college student with a desire to go into med-school. Margot had been the one to convince him into doing so. That meant he would have less desire to have an active role in the family company.

This was something that her parents obviously were of two minds about. On the one hand, this meant that their wayward son would be a doctor. On the other hand, it meant that their child would not be working with them. Margot thought it was all hypocritical.

They had spent all her childhood running around hell's half acre on adventures and then spent all Nial's childhood leaving him at home to be raised by her practically. They were then blaming her specifically when he would misbehave and blame her for sending him off to boarding school. She was a teenager and should not have been left alone with him, to begin with. Especially not for months on end.

Margot often wondered what people would have thought about the beloved couple Nadia and Brandon had they lived with them. Her mother was adventure crazy. Adventure crazy enough that she had accidentally gotten her own father kidnapped a half a dozen times for months on end. She had no idea how the company survived in the '70s and '80s without her being an active part of it. The CEO of a fortune five hundred company being MIA every other damn month was not a good thing.

"Hey, Margie!" Nial said.

She shot him a look but smiled, "Hey, kid." She messed up his hair. Nial was the only person that she allowed to screw up her name. She was Margot to everyone else. It was that simple. If it weren't, she would come for your head.

The door opened, and it was her step-cousin Vivica along with her mother, Gail. Why on earth did they still humor these two? Her uncle was long gone at this point. It might have sounded harsh, but she felt like they both were gold diggers. Nadia immediately ran over to the two of them and gave them big hugs.

"Oh, Gail, you wore the dress we saw at the store last week. I told you that it would look great on you!" Nadia smiled. The difference in her tone was obnoxious in Margot's mind.

"Vivica, you look wonderful as well. It's so nice to have you in town for the holiday. You need to come around more often. Your mother and I both miss you."

Vivica looked pissed off, "Well, I mean, we will see. I really have nothing left in Grosse Pointe since my bitch of a sister married my fiancé," Vivica said as if it was something normal to state in a public setting.

Nial walked over to Vivica with a smile on his face, "Hey

Vivica, how have you been?"

"Oh, just wonderful other than my bitch of an absentee sister coming back into my life after all these years to steel the only man I've ever loved," Vivica said bitterly.

"Tell us how you really feel, dear!" Margot said, overly chipper.

The redheaded Weston girl looked at Nial, "Will you take me to fix a drink before I rip your sister's head off?"

CLIFF — APRIL 1990

It was so weird for Cliff to be back at North Pointe after four years of finally getting the heck out of his childhood family home. He had always hated living there, but his grandmother Delia insisted that he should move back in ever since he married Tiffany. Once Tiffany had heard the offer, she had insisted herself. Cliff wanted to keep Tiffany happy and agreed, even if it meant having to be around his father, Rodrick. He did like being around his younger sister Phyllis more often, though.

"Sister, have you seen the large blue bowl?" he asked sister Mary Newman, as he prepared to set the table for dinner that night. Sister Mary Newman had been hired on as Phyllis' nanny after retiring from teaching the year before. It was also insistent upon his grandmother, who happened to be best friends with the nun.

33

Mary smiled, "Cliff, how many times do I have to remind you that you can call me Mary outside of the church," as she playfully hit him over the head.

He had to admit that since Mary had moved in, his grandmother seemed a lot happier. The backdoor opened, and Tiffany walked in. Cliff thought she was beautiful, and yet it was hard for him to smile around her, which is why he was so insistent on keeping her happy. It was so different than being with Vivica. Tiffany made dinner or helped with dinner every night. She was still studying for her med degree at the same time. She dressed conservatively. She belonged to Mrs. Templeton's book club and insisted they attend church every Sunday. It was the opposite of Vivica, where every time she wasn't away modeling, she would be hiding in bed or insist on going out to eat for all their meals.

"Hi, Tiffany." Within the last few weeks, he realized that he still spoke to Tiffany as if she were a new friend and not a lover and definitely not a wife. It was just so odd. Yet, there was something about Tiffany that just felt so familiar.

It was the way that Vivica was when he first had met her. Cliff had to remind himself constantly that he was twelve when they had first met. She was such a different person back then. They both were. They had grown so much, and it seemed to be in different directions. That is what he constantly told himself, at least.

"You will not believe the fun my study group and I had together today," she smiled. Tiffany had a great smile. It could be threatening, though. That's what Phyliss kept saying, at least.

Cliff had to admit that he could see it.

Cliff sat down at the kitchen table. "Well, that is wonderful," he thought out loud.

"I told them all that I would be inviting them over very soon for dinner. I can't wait to show off our amazing house!"

Tiffany smiled yet again. She walked over to him and gave him a kiss on the head, "I have to go get changed. I'm shadowing in the ER tonight!"

He wanted to process what she had just said a little bit better when his grandmother walked in from the hallway. "I suppose it is nice that she considers this her house already.

Vivica always made sure that throw pillow in the living room was always in the exact same place when she left," Delia sat down.

This was pretty much exactly what he was thinking. Vivica was always freaked out about being in the Knight house. Tiffany had already started to remodel certain rooms. She had tried to throw out the desk in his childhood bedroom, but he refused. She had insisted on moving to a room at the end of the hall that was slightly larger. Really it was only slightly. It was also closer to his father's room, which he found unsettling for any number of reasons. Yet, he continued to say yes to whatever Tiffany wanted. "I'm glad that she enjoys it here. Really I do…"

"She isn't anything like her sister, though," Delia pointed out.

Cliff sighed, "No, she is not."

Delia sighed, "Cliff, it is not too late to back out of this marriage. I always had my reservations about Vivica. She was loud, abrasive, and related to the Bloom family. I have no issue with the Fitzpatrick's. It's just the whole Bloom-Brash family that I was never big on. Sorry to get off-topic. Regardless, I think you were happier with Vivica, and I think you should be with the person you are happiest with."

She was not wrong. He did not know for certain that the woman that he was happiest with was indeed Vivica. He only went on dates before Vivica. He never actually dated anyone seriously. Cliff supposed that had to do with Vivica always vetoing all the girls he would have crushes on before they had gotten together.

Cliff technically had not even really dated Tiffany. They had innocently flirted with one another a few times before they ended up married. Cliff knew looking back he should have thought about the situation further. There was no backing out, though. At least, he did not think that there was.

VIVICA – JANUARY 2019

"I'm coming!" screamed Vivica as she walked out of the drawing-room and into the foyer of North Pointe. It was a hell of a time for Holly to be using the bathroom, Vivica thought. Then again, there was a staff of like thirty or something in this house, yet they were not answering the door, which would not stop ringing.

She took a deep breath and opened the door. "What?" she screamed. The redhead looked at who was at the door and stepped back. "Oh, good lord, it's you."

Jackie Carson-Costa. A woman who was in disturbingly good shape with golden blonde hair and green eyes. She was always smelled drenched in Chanel No.5 and had no fashion sense whatsoever.

"You going to let me in, Red?" she said in her thick

Brooklyn accent. Vivica could hear her chewing on a piece of gum loudly.

Was she going to? Yes. Did she want to? Hell no! Jackie hated women. Vivica had issues with certain women, but she got along with enough people. Jackie hated all women, including her own damn daughter. She knew this interaction was bound to happen sooner rather than later. "Well, please come in."

"I think you know why I'm here," Jackie said loudly.

"Yes… Harry and your son," Vivica said. She was shocked that it took this long for Jackie to come to her to talk about her child and Harry's relationship. "They make a cute couple."

The mob wife looked around, "Yeah, they do. So, you are going to do a better job at making them feel comfortable around here."

"What on earth do you mean?" Vivica asked. She had been kind to Preston over the last few months. Sure, there were a few instances, including attempting to sabotage them going to a school dance together.

She had also tried setting both boys up with different men. She even had considered hiring a hooker, but Holly hid her bank information for a week to stop her. Other than that, she had been very supportive.

Vivica then remembered the time she stole Harry's phone last week in an attempt to break them up. It was possible that Jackie might have found out about the incident.

Really though, Vivica had moved on from trying to

break up the two boys. "I am supportive of Harry dating men or whatever he chooses to date. His father keeps mentioning a couch. I'd be protesting on the street if he wanted to marry a couch!"

The blonde rolled her eyes. Vivica really could not stand this woman. "I will not let you play with my son's emotions fire crotch! I've let a lot of things slide over the years, but you mess with my son, and bitch you will make an enemy out of me!"

Vivica had to be honest and admit that she thought they were enemies already. "Well, is there anything else you would like to discuss? I have a wedding to plan. It's right around the corner, and I have friends coming in out of the yin yang. Between my childhood best friend Brianna Belle, my early twenties bestie Bridget Madwell, and my maid, there is about to be a power battle for who gets to be the maid of honor."

Someone once again knocked on the door. "Damn it, Holly…" Vivica groaned.

She went to open the door and once again she could not believe her eyes. "Red! Surprise! I know we are a few weeks early, but I just couldn't wait to see you!" Ironically enough, it was Bridget Madwell and her daughter Amanda. She had not seen Amanda in a few years now.

"Bridget!" Vivica screamed. She rushed and gave her a hug. Vivica then turned around and looked at Jackie. "Oh, um Jackie, this is Bridget. I can't honestly remember if you two have met."

Bridget leaned into Vivica's ear. "Vivica, isn't that lady a mob wife?"

"Hey!" Screamed Jackie. "Ok, a show of hands; who here hasn't been accused of killing someone."

The four women all stood silent for a second. Amanda then raised her hand. "Not yet…"

"I'm so glad that you brought Amanda with you," Vivica said. She honestly was very happy.

This was all part of her plan. Vivica once again looked at Jackie. "Look, I have some catching up to do with my dear friend. If you don't mind coming back later?" Vivica said.

Jackie gave her a nasty look and headed towards the door, shouldering Bridget. "Alright bitch. Just know this ain't over. It ain't over by a long shot. Jackie walked out the front door and left.

"What on earth was that about?" Bridget asked.

Amanda laughed, "Oh good. You want me to live here where there are a bunch of crime lords…" Amanda rolled her eyes.

"Live here?" Vivica asked.

The brunette modeling executive sighed, "Well, thank you, Amanda, for getting to the point. One of the reasons we are here so early is that Amanda has an interview at the boarding school that Brad used to go to," Bridget explained. She put her hand on her hips. "Amanda was expelled for selling drugs at her last school. This is her last chance otherwise, she gets to go to public school."

Amanda rolled her eyes. "Bridget, I wasn't expelled for selling drugs. I was expelled for telling my classmates that I was selling them drugs when I was really selling them laxatives and Advil. It's not my fault that those idiots decided to act like lunatics..."

Vivica looked at Bridget, "She calls you by your first name?"

"She isn't supposed to," Bridget explained.

The redhead had a plan to put Amanda and Brad together. It was her last resort to getting rid of Lucas Entertainment once and for all from her sons' life. "I can't wait for Amanda and Brad to hang out again like when they were younger! Harry too! Amanda, do you have any single LGBT friends?" Bridget and Amanda both looked at Vivica in complete confusion.

LUCY-JANUARY 2019

The blonde took a deep breath as she opened the door to her old new house. It had been odd to move back into what was Austin's home. Lucy felt it was bizarre and a bit kismet to share a connection with Vivica, who had grown up in the house, as well as her stepfather, DJ, and even Nadia Fitzpatrick, who had lived here for some time.

Vivica had made sure the house was refurnished after having already been cleaned up and painted. She walked into the house, and it was oddly silent. Xander was still at work, and Langley was with Harry getting ready for Vivica's engagement party, which she was supposed to be doing as well. It was not that she did not want to go to her friend's engagement party. It was that she was tired.

Perry walked downstairs in a pair of tan dress slacks, a

blue button-down and pink tie, and brown leather dress shoes. His red hair was slicked back. Perry looked hot Lucy thought,

"So, how was work?"

Perry semi-agreed to move in with her after only a few months of dating. Sure, he could afford to live by himself, and he had his room at the Fitzpatrick mansion, but Margot was driving him up a wall more than she had when he was growing up.

Work was just peaches and cream, "Your mother wants me to be her damn clone or something. Is it because we are dating?" Lucy asked out loud. She wondered if that was too embracive of a question.

"Probably... The thing is that you are the first girl that Joshua and I have ever dated that she has semi-liked, which is both a good thing for me and a bad thing for you. Though that said, she doesn't think that I'm good enough for you."

Lucy looked at him in confusion, "How on earth are you not good enough for me?"

"While you might have gotten your degree from money, you've been busting your ass for six years. Plus, you have been working with her worst enemy on the planet. That gives you a boost because it means you must be hardworking," Perry pointed out.

It was great that Margot liked her. Lucy sort of liked Margot to some degree. To some degree, she was definitely a bitch, though. "I'm so tired. The damn hotel's night manager is a train wreck and was asking me a thousand questions for two hours. I need to go and get ready."

"Do you want some company in the shower?"

The blonde executive looked at her red-haired hunk.

"You look like you are all ready to go."

"It takes five minutes for me to get all of this back on and only ten seconds to take it all off." Perry gave her a dirty but sexy smile.

Lucy gestured to him to follow her up the stairs. She stopped him with her hand about halfway up. She took her hair out of the bun it was in and slid her sweater off. Perry quickly unbuttoned his shirt and removed his tie. He looked at her very sensually, "Come on before Manhattan Barbie and GPPD Ken get home." She laughed, and the two ran upstairs.

HANNAH – JANUARY 2020

"Can I please see Xander Kingsley?" Hannah Knight asked. He was supposed to pick her up from Knight over an hour ago, which she had insisted he did not need to do considering she had a car. She was worried because she had not heard from him pretty much since the night before. The desk clerk pointed back to where he was. Hannah could see him working on something. "Hi, Xander," she said.

Xander looked up and looked at his watch, "Oh wow… Sorry. I had so much paperwork. Holly's husband usually hands it off to me. Ranking and what have you. I totally forgot I said I wanted to pick you up. How long before the engagement party?"

Hannah sighed, "Not long, and it isn't the engagement party. It's just a get together of the family." Her aunt insisted on having a pre-dinner before the guests started to show up within the next few weeks for the wedding.

It was going to be a wreck; she already knew it. The bridesmaid dresses were a disaster. Her sister Hope never responded to her father's message about the wedding. Then her cousin Laura was MIA as always. She knew that her aunt had an odd parenting style when it came to Laura with her uncle Nial, but it was still weird to hold a grudge for as long as she had.

"Right, not an engagement party… Langley keeps calling it an engagement party," Xander explained as he stood up.

"Is it ok for you to even leave right now? It's totally ok if you have to stay," she explained. She understood, and again it wasn't that big of a deal. She probably would only get a few minutes to spend with her aunt or father all evening. The bulk of the evening would be spent listening to Xander's little sister Langley reciting one-liners and the inevitable visit from Mrs. Templeton even though no one invited her."

Xander grabbed his phone, "I have to be back at three. I can't stay at the party for long, but I made a promise to you, Hannah, and I'm sticking to it," he spoke. He wrote a little note for his partner, "Alright, I'll meet you at North Pointe, in like two hours?"

Hannah smiled, "Yeah, around then." Things were really changing with Xander. He was actually committed to her. That might have been one of the reasons her sister was not going to be there that night, or at the wedding for that matter… "Alright. I'll see you in a little bit."

LANGLEY – JAUNUARY 2019

The door to Harry's room opened, and it was Brad. Langley turned around and smiled. "You should have knocked! We could have been naked," she joked.

Brad took a minute to smile. Langley almost forgot that she and Harry had sex back in May. It was right after he had been outed as gay online from a sex tape that the person he lost his virginity to had posted. Brad had found them right after. "Well, I've seen both of you naked enough times that I don't think there is anything to hide," he winked at her. Langley took that as a sign that he was getting a little more into the idea of them finally taking it to the next step. She would take him feeling her up at this point.

"Well, anytime you want to see more, I'm into it!" Langley said.

"I'm standing right here," Harry said quietly.

Langley shrugged, "We have been over this Harry talk loud and proud. If not proud, then at least assert yourself. Such as the time I got my name on the Hermes VIP list over that good-for-nothing reality star."

Harry nodded his head, "I'll try to remember."

"So, this is what I'm going to wear tonight," she told the two boys. She was wearing a blue turtleneck with a black pleated skirt and boots. Her hair was higher than Dolly Parton, and all the drag queens of New York City combined. If Brad says that it's too revealing or that her outfit shows too much skin, she was going to scream.

The football player smiled at her. "You look great," he said without too much emphasis. Which meant that she was well dressed enough but clearly could have tried better. Langley would crack the code eventually, she thought.

"Where is Preston?" Langley asked, having a tone that sounded rather annoyed. She wanted Brad to sense the tone, but he seemed unbothered by it, which annoyed her even more.

Harry picked his phone up. "Apparently, he is on his way," Harry continued to read through the text. "Oh no..."

"What?" Brad asked him.

"Jackie Costa was over today," Harry explained.

Brad's eyes widened. "Oh shit... I didn't see my mom downstairs or at our house."

The Kingsley girl looked at the two of them. "You two are acting like Preston's mom shot Vivica…"

The two cousins looked at her as their faces turned white.

"Oh, Christ," Harry said. Which was out of character, Langley thought.

Brad ran out the door and clearly was headed towards the grand staircase. Harry followed after him, and Langley, just sort of, walked out along with them. It wasn't that she wasn't worried. It was that Vivica clearly hated her, and also, she doubted that Jackie killed Vivica. In New York, Langley had been around enough mob families to know when someone had been killed.

Brad ran down the staircases and headed left for the drawing-room. He stopped at the doorway, with Harry stopping along with him. Langley managed to get to the bottom of the stairs herself finally. "Will the two of you please slow the hell down?" She had never seen Harry run so fast in her life.

"Amanda Madwell?" Brad said with a smile on his face.

Amanda Madwell? Langley had heard that name before. Amanda Madwell… Why was that name so familiar? She walked over to the door and peaked in. "Amanda Madwell," Langley screamed from across the room.

"Will someone please tell Lotus to use her inside voice?" Vivica asked.

Amanda walked up to the three other teens. She gave Brad and Harry a group hug. "Oh my gosh! It's been too long!"

Brad turned to Langley. "Langley, this is Amanda! She lived here up until she was like four. I only ever get to see her whenever my mom is in LA or New York nowadays."

The brunette girl looked at Langley and laughed.

"Kingsley... My how the mighty have fallen?"

Langley started to turn red, "Amanda... The last time I saw you, I believe you were expelled for having an inappropriate relationship with our math teacher?"

Bridget sighed from the other room, "How does she know about that? I paid the papers to keep their traps shut."

The Madwell daughter laughed again, "Oh, relax, mother. Kingsley and I used to be classmates back in the day."

Brad, Harry, and even Vivica all looked at Langley in shock. "You and Amanda used to go to school together? Such a small world," Harry said.

Go to school? Yeah, sure, that is what she would call it. Langley was the head bitch of her grade on her way to being the top bitch of the school, just as Lucy had been back in the day. Amanda showed up from an upstate boarding school and wreaked havoc on the entire student body. She slept with all the boys and pissed off all the girls. Out of all the people that Langley knew would one day come back into her life, this girl was not one of them.

Vivica stood up, "Bridget and Amanda are back in town a few weeks early for the wedding. Isn't that nice? It will give Brad and Amanda so much time to catch up!"

The Madwell girl had managed to sleep with almost every boy in the school, including two teachers. She only got caught sleeping with the one after the guy's wife found them together. Langley loved sex. Amanda needed sex. Amanda had known Brad since they were born, it would seem. Langley looked at Vivica, and Vivica shot her a look that said it all. The blonde girl walked straight over to Brad and gave him a tight hug. "Amanda, it's a small world. Brad and I are dating," and that wasn't about to change.

MARGOT – JANUARY 2019

"I'm firing whatever maid I see first! How hard is it to get the damn door?" Margot screamed as she walked into the foyer. She looked out the peephole and grunted. Reluctantly, the CEO opened the door, "What the hell are you doing here?"

Nial walked in, "Anthony Costa…"

"Come in," Margot said, annoyed.

"Why on earth is my key not working?" Nial asked.

The two walked into the library. "I had the keys changed. I didn't want your ex-wife getting in. Don't worry, I gave one to Brad but told him it would be revoked if she found it." Margot sat down, and Nial followed. "So, how long are you going to be in town?"

The younger brother shrugged, "I don't know, for a few

weeks. I have to keep an eye on a few of Costa's men. There was a bad shootout, and a few of them are wounded."

"You do realize that the Whore from Beverly Hills is marrying Cliff in a few weeks, right?" Margot looked at her younger brother. Anthony Costa had a lot of pull in what Nial did, but even so, Nial could have recommended another doctor. Nial knew damn well that Vivica was getting married. "Nial, you better not be thinking of trying to win her back. She can't be Vivica- Weston – Fitzpatrick – Knight – Fitzpatrick – Fitzpatrick – Fitzpatrick. I'm not letting her move back in. I've changed her room into a storage closet."

"You mean my room?" Nial asked.

Margot rolled her eyes, "Not the point. Either way, do what you came to do but do not get involved with that wedding. Leave the Whore alone. If Cliff Knight wants to ruin his life with her, that is his business. You will not get involved. You two are terrible together. Absolutely terrible."

VIVICA – APRIL 1990

Did Nial ever shut up? Vivica asked herself as she continued to nurse her third rum and coke. He talked about three things, school, Anthony Costa, and sports. None of those things interested her. It didn't help that he spoke in a flirtatious tone and kept getting closer and closer to her. Luckily, his nephew Joshua kept showing him new things that he was drawing every five minutes. Vivica felt bad for Joshua and baby Perry. They had Margot as a mother.

"So, did you happen to catch any of the b-ball games last month?" Nial asked her.

"I was in Paris," Vivica rolled her eyes.

"Woah... Wow, it's been a few years since I've been there. What were you up to there?"

She had been modeling lingerie, but she wasn't about to tell him that. "Just a modeling gig."

Nial smiled, "Nice! I always tell my friends up at school that we are technically related." He coughed, "I mean obviously not by blood, though."

Vivica nodded, "Unfortunately, not." She had never in her life wanted to be blood-related to DJ Brash let him rest in peace, but at this moment in time, she wished she had been. Though, something told her that Nial would still be hitting on her right now. "I wonder what they are doing at the North Pointe tonight?" Vivica said.

Brandon Fitzpatrick walked in and scoffed, "Probably drinking the blood of their enemies."

Nadia followed him in, "Well, we are all here, but then again, they have so many enemies who can keep track."

Ever since Vivica and Cliff's engagement had broken off, Brandon and Nadia had taken it as a sign for open season on the Knight family, which in large said more about how they too felt for her bitch of a sister. They considered her one of them but not Tiffany, which in retrospect was a scary thing. Vivica being considered a Fitzpatrick made her have goosebumps, but not in a good way.

"They aren't all bad," Vivica said. Then again, Cliff had backstabbed her. "I mean, Phyliss is a good kid," Vivica quickly added.

"Oh, give her five years. She will be just as reckless as the other Knight's. I don't know how Sister Mary Newman puts up with them. I suppose Delia isn't the worst, but neither of her children turned out so great," Nadia explained.

Brandon laughed. "Oh lord, do you remember Clifton and Dallas back in school? They were always in detention. They ran off to Amsterdam the moment Clifton's trust fund kicked in at twenty-two. That's why Delia raised the age for Cliff and now Phyliss."

"Clifton was bad, but none of us need to be reminded about how horrible Rodrick was back in the day. He has only gotten worse since then," Nadia reminded them.

Margot walked in. "Rodrick isn't that bad, mother."

Vivica wondered if Nadia and Brandon knew about Margot's affair with Rodrick back when Vivica was sixteen. She discovered it herself the night that DJ was killed in the accident. Vivica found that a little unsettling to connect the two things. Either way, she was sick of listening to all of them talk horribly of Cliff. The only person who was allowed to do that right now was her. At least that was what she kept telling herself.

Nial grabbed her hand, "Come on, Viv, let's go take a walk." Viv? Did he just call her Viv? Vivica hated being called Viv, but at the same time, she was glad that someone could sense she needed to get out of the situation.

The two walked out of the library and then out of the foyer onto the street. "Thanks," Vivica said.

"Yeah, no problem... I mean, I'm no fan of the Knight

family myself, but I can tell that you are still adjusting to a world where they weren't a staple in your life," Nial explained.

That was probably the most mature thing that Nial had ever told Vivica. "I just don't know how to adjust. Realistically, once Easter is over, I suppose I'll be back in New York, LA, or somewhere in Europe."

"I hear that Australia is a nice place to hide out," Nial told her.

Vivica shuttered, "Oh lord no... bad experience with Bridget Dante and Australia. Never again."

"Have you thought about enrolling in school?" Nial wondered.

Aside from Gail and Cliff insisting that it would help her out, she just never saw the use. Especially once she started to make money from modeling. The fact was that she was one of the highest-paid models in the world at the moment.

Between the paycheck she got from posing for a singular magazine and her trust fund from both her father and mother's family that would kick in by the time she was thirty, it made no sense to waste her time in a college setting. What was she going to get out of it? She had the basic money skills to know how to save.

Cliff and his step-grandfather had taught her well. Myles Madwell was also wonderful at helping her invest properly. She was twenty-three years old and already set for at least the next decade and could splurge within her means.

College would mean being stuck in a classroom for months on end again and then thousands in student loans. Which, yes, she could pay back, but no, she had no desire to do so for a degree that she might never even use. "I'm good."

Nial shrugged, "I don't know. I mean, school has been fine so far for me."

The redhead turned to the blonde boy, "What possessed you to go for a medical degree?" She never really thought that he had much interest in that sort of thing. Then again, she never paid much interest in him at all.

"I mean… more or less to prove myself, plus I don't want to take over for the company one day when my dad retires. Margot is already set to do so, and I want her to," Nial said.

"I don't understand Margot at all." Vivica rolled her eyes.

"Oh, she is everything that you probably think of her and more, but she was there for me growing up. She visited while I was at boarding school. It was her choice to put me there, and I have to say that I think it was for the best. I needed stability, and Margot wasn't ready to raise a child while my parents ran around the world playing super spy," Nial told her.

It always shocked Vivica that the Fitzpatrick's had such a bizarre home life. DJ was definitely Nadia's brother, but he was just so much more about family. Something she regretted not appreciating while he was alive. Whereas Nadia and Brandon were all about adventure and chasing the next one into the sunset.

There was no proof, and no one ever spoke of it, but Vivica often wondered if Nadia and Brandon ever even wanted children or if they did, but then realized that they wanted adventure and fun first. They had been a good aunt and uncle to her though over the years. Even back when DJ was alive and Nadia used to feud with her mother, they had always treated her well.

"I still just don't see you as being a doctor." She thought about what she said for a moment and then stopped walking,

"I didn't mean for that to come out the way it did."

Nial smiled, "It's fine. None of my friends seem to support me. Margot is the only one who seems to be super supportive. I guess your mom too. She always sends the most awesome care packages up at school."

Vivica had no idea that her mother had been doing that. It made her wonder if she would have done the same thing for her or why she had been doing that for her bitch of a sister. It didn't matter. Vivica was on a strict diet, and her mother's cookies were too addicting. She already spent three hours at the gym.

"We should probably start heading back. Dinner will be ready soon enough," Nial pointed out, and the two turned back in the opposite direction of where they had been walking.

CLIFF – JANUARY 2019

The day had been long, and if he were honest, he could have lived without this family dinner. It was more or less just a taste test for what could be served at the wedding in a few weeks. Still, he promised Weston, and he was going to follow through. Lord only knew that he didn't want to, though, and just wanted to sit on the couch and watch TV while he put off work that would still need to be done when dinner was over.

He got out of his car in the family garage and found Hannah still in her car texting. He knocked on her window, and she rolled it down, "Are you alright?"

Hannah turned to him, "Yeah. I was just looking into the money that we are still trying to recover from KMC."

Cliff wished that they could have just forgotten about all of that, but lord knows his father probably ensured that he could discover it the moment he died. Rodrick was known to be that kind of a jackass.

"Well, we can talk about it more after dinner. You still need to get dressed, and I still need to get dressed, said Cliff.

The daughter got out of her car, "I suppose you are right. I just needed a short distraction, I suppose."

"What's wrong? Is this about Xander again? I don't know if I like that boy, to be completely honest."

Hannah sighed, "Yes and no. He just works a lot now, which I suppose is a good thing, but I'd rather he spends more time with me than at the GPPD."

Cliff had to admit that he wasn't fond of a police officer dating his daughter. The GPPD and the Knight family were never known for having a great relationship. There was a reason why Rodrick constantly donated so much damn money to them over the years. It kept them off his case. He needed to stop thinking about his damn father. Rodrick was dead, and he wasn't coming back.

"Is he coming tonight?" Cliff asked.

His daughter nodded, "For a little bit at least. I told him he didn't have to come, but he insisted. I don't know."

"I'm glad that you have found someone," Cliff said. He knew it was an awkward thing for him to be happy when he had been with Hope first. Though, Hope supposedly broke up with him and then ran off to Europe.

"You are just happy that I'm not dating a hipster in Royal Oak anymore," Hannah crossed her arms.

Cliff shuddered at the notion. "Hannah, that man had no job and smelled." He realized that was too broad a defense because there were multiple men who matched that description that she happened to have dated. Luckily, none of them were ever invited back to their house at the time.

This was mostly because Hannah had not been on great terms with him or her mother.

"Hannah, did you stay away because of me?" He realized that asking this question was almost out of line. "I mean, you do know that I've always supported you as a person. Right?"

He realized that even saying that was sort of untrue. When Tiffany had returned from being *dead*, she very much took a liking to Hope's life over Hannah's. Hope was the popular cheerleader that wanted to be a doctor in honor of her mother. Cliff, in reality, saw nothing wrong with that.

Harry had once mentioned something called heteronormality. It was used to describe how people did things based on how heterosexuals had conducted society for so long instead of realizing that there were alternatives. Cliff wondered if, in a way, this applied to how he treated Hannah. He already knew it applied to Harry, obviously, considering he just always assumed he was into girls.

Hannah wanted to be an artist and wanted to be different though he just assumed that Hannah wanted what her sister wanted. The irony is, Cliff never wanted the things that his father wanted for him, which were all the things that Tiffany seemed to want for the family.

Tiffany had been the one to decide they would move into North Pointe. When he and Vivica had started to become more serious, they had made it a point to plan out their future. One thing they had both agreed on at the time was that they never wanted to live at the Knight family home in marriage. Yet, Tiffany's insistence shoved him into living there his entire life aside from college.

Cliff and Vivica had also said they would make money for themselves instead of relying on the Knight's money. Tiffany liked not having student loans, showing off the newest Knight car, and having the best of the best in terms of clothing.

Vivica was self-made ironically enough. Tiffany had studied her ass off to get where she was in school. That wasn't to say that she had ever had to slum it. She had her father's money attached to her the entire time. Vivica never had that support from her father because her mother wouldn't allow it even in her twenties, which was fine considering that Vivica made ridiculously good money as a model.

"I'll see you inside, Hannah," Cliff said as he got out his phone. He went to his phone contacts and found Tiffany's number. He hit the call button after a moment of hesitation. The phone kept ringing and ringing, and it eventually went to voicemail. Cliff realized that it was either really late or earlier or whatever in Europe. He wasn't even sure why he was calling his ex-wife. Cliff made a mistake with Tiffany. He knew that now.

CLIFF – APRIL 1990

It was starting to resonate with him that his family was not fans of his new wife. He had no idea what he wanted if he was honest with himself. Vivica was his first love. Tiffany was his wife. There weren't many other girls in-between, and maybe that was the overall issue. He couldn't deny it. Cliff Knight was in love with two sisters. An abrasive redhead who spoke her mind but wanted what was best for those around her. Then there was the brunet doctor who wanted to be the perfect wife in addition to that.

Facts were facts. His grandmother was bound to not like whoever he was married to. She wasn't that big of a fan of Vivica either. She more or less wanted him to be with the perfect Latina woman that just didn't exist. It was more or less the truth. Delia had always joked that she had hoped that he would marry a Latina to spite his great-grandfather Heathcliff.

His younger sister was a different story altogether. She was too young to have a choice in the matter. She loved Vivica so much because she came first. Tiffany treated her just as well. He wasn't concerned about that.

Sister Mary Newman was a nun. She wasn't allowed to have an opinion, and in his mind, he never really thought that she was fond of Vivica.

Gail was a wildcard. Yes, she was their mother, but he had only ever known her as Vivica's male best friend and later boyfriend. It definitely would be hard to adjust.

The Knight man walked up the staircase of Saint Agnes. The school he had gone to from pre-school to his senior year of high school. He was back to volunteer for an event. He was the Knight family ambassador. He looked up from the ground and noticed a familiar redhead walking by. She also looked up and smiled but then frowned. Cliff started to run towards her,

"Vivica... Wait!"

Vivica turned to look at him, "What do you want, Cliff?"

"I didn't realize that you were back in town," he explained.

The redhaired Weston sighed, "I suppose that my sister wouldn't have mentioned it after coming by last night."

Cliff honestly had no idea. Tiffany had a tendency not to tell him where she was going, which he supposed was her prerogative. "How was Europe?"

"I was in Beverly Hills, actually. I'm meeting Bridget at

the end of next week in New York, though. From there, we will be going off to Paris, London, Copenhagen, and Milan. The whole tour. I won't be around much this summer. Which I suppose is fine for you."

This was not ok for him. Or was it? He had no idea what his answer was supposed to be on that subject. "We really need to hang out before you leave."

Vivica gave him the most bizarre look, "I have no idea why you think I would want to spend time with you? We aren't together anymore."

Yeah, they weren't. It was killing him not to spend time with her.

"Vivica, you are my best friend in the world. Do you remember back in middle school? You, Brianna Belle, and I were the three Musketeers. Everyone used to joke about it."

She rolled her eyes, "Well, I suppose that Brianna might want to talk with you, but she moved to the West Coast a while back." She brushed her back, "I actually did spend some good quality time with her though while I was out that way. She doesn't want to talk with you either."

Of course, she didn't. She actually called and cursed him out when he left Vivica. He had never heard her swear before.

"I can't have you in my life, Weston."

Someone walked up to the two of them. He faintly recognized the boy. He then remembered who it was, "Nial Fitzpatrick? What on earth are you doing here?"

Nial looked at Vivica, who was clearly hurt. "Is he bothering you, Vivica?"

He looked at the way that Nial was holding on to Vivica.

"Aren't the two of you cousins?"

"Step-Cousins… and I don't know what you are implying," Vivica snapped at him. She looked at Nial, "Come on, let's go inside." She took his hand.

Cliff had no idea what was going on, but he could tell that a storm was brewing. The light at the end of that storm was not going to be easy to reach.

NIAL – JANUARY 2019

It was nice to be home, the doctor thought to himself. Even if his sister had literally redone the entire house in her own style, he walked into the library where his sister was drinking a cup of tea. "What do mom and dad think about all of this?"

Margot shrugged, and looked up at him from her tablet, "I have no idea and don't personally care. They live in Florida."

Nial crossed his arms and continued to look at her, "They had always been very nostalgic about the look of the house."

"You literally pissed all over the walls as a child that we had to repaint," she sighed. "You are being overly dramatic."

The doorbell rang, and the two siblings looked at one another. "I'll get it."

"Well, I sure as hell wasn't about to get it," Margot stated.

He walked back into the foyer and looked through the peephole. Nial opened the door. "Jackie! And Anthony. So, great to see you both!" He knew that they would be coming over eventually. It wasn't as if he was afraid of either of them. It was that he knew that owing either of them a favor was always a disaster in the making. "Well, come on in!"

Margot walked out from the library and put a smile on her face. "Well, if it isn't the Costa's!" she said, looking at Nial.

Nial knew that Margot wasn't a giant fan of them as a couple. She adored Anthony, but Jackie was a handful. Nial didn't know many women who enjoyed being around Jackie. It was world war three when Vivica and Jackie would have to be in the same room. He never could tell who she disliked more, Jackie or Tiffany.

"Well, if it isn't the second most beautiful woman in Grosse pointe? How have you been?" Anthony kissed Margot on the cheek.

"Busy… so busy. Why has it been so long since you two have been over?" Margot looked at Jackie, who was most definitely chewing on gum. She rolled her eyes.

Jackie gave a fake smile to Margot, "So, you two weren't invited to the weird already engaged and set to wed party for Red and Mr. Motor City himself?"

Nial bit at his cheek a little bit, "Uh, no… I don't think they even know that I am back from Europe as of yet. I plan to reach out to Brad tomorrow, though." He wasn't entirely sure if his son would want to speak with him. He needed to make sure that Brad knew that he was there for him, though. Nial wasn't about to let Cliff be the primary father figure for his son.

His hatred for Cliff made people turn heads. How dare he hate the saint of Grosse Pointe? People really loved to rewrite history as time went on.

"So, I'm sure you have heard that your kid brother is doing some work for an associate and me?" Anthony asked Margot.

"I've known Nial long enough to know that when he comes home, he wants something, and normally I somehow get involved," as she shot him an extremely dirty look.

Nial laughed it off, "Oh, you know how we are, two peas in a pod." He playfully punched Margot in the shoulder. She smacked him back.

VIVICA – JANUARY 2019

C liff walked into their shared bedroom at North Pointe and kissed her on the forehead. She turned around from her vanity and started to kiss him passionately herself, "Hello, Mister Knight."

"Hello, soon to be Mrs. Knight," Cliff said back.

She had to admit that it had a nice ring to it. "So, I have some great news. We have two people joining us for dinner."

Her fiancé smiled, "Oh, really, who could those two people be? Did you manage to track down Hope and Laura?"

Well, there was Cliff being over-enthusiastic. Vivica laughed nervously. "Uh, nope... Bridget and her daughter Amanda. You know how much you love Bridget."

Cliff's smile turned into a frown, "Oh, God help us.

Please tell me she isn't here to take you galivanting across Europe again."

She knew that he couldn't stand Bridget, but he also knew that she would be at the wedding regardless. So, Vivica felt like he would be able to get over it faster. "I put them up at my house."

"I suppose we will have to live with it. Just promise me you won't take any modeling jobs until we are back from our honeymoon," he stated to her.

That was definitely fair, "It's a deal. Though, your loss because I could have gotten us a free vacation out of me modeling somewhere."

Cliff rolled his eyes, "You realize we have all the money in the world to go on as many vacations as we want, right?"

"Let me remind you, Clifton Knight, the Third, that not when we were twelve, not when we started dating, not when we thought we were married last time did I ever expect a singular dollar out of you. Your money is not why I love you," Vivica said very loudly. She didn't mean to go over the edge, but for years she was deemed a gold digger for dating Cliff, for marrying Nial and Luke. The only time she ever got married was when Nial discovered money that they were both entitled to but only could collect if they were still married. This resulted in her second failed marriage to the blonde doctor. It was one of her biggest regrets.

The Knight CEO gave her a kiss, "That's what I've always loved about you. I knew from the first day that I met

72

you that you weren't after my name."

She kissed him back, "No. I was after your beautiful blue eyes." She started to unbutton his shirt, and she could feel his heart racing. "Go take a shower and get ready. The dinner will start soon."

"Care to join me?" Cliff asked.

Vivica sighed. "I literally got a blow-out today. I'm not about to redo my hair by myself."

Cliff shrugged and continued to take off his shirt. He then slipped his pants and briefs off and walked into the bathroom. "Enjoy the view..."

"I always do," Vivica rolled her eyes.

NIAL – APRIL 1990

It was known to pretty much everyone that he always had a crush on his semi-step-cousin Vivica. Yet, he grew up and moved on with many different women, so many that it was hard to count.

"Nial... Did you want to go to the diner for something to eat?" Vivica asked him.

The Med-Student woke up from his fantasy. "Oh, um, I suppose." He had to admit that he still wanted Vivica. He also had to wonder if the reason that he wanted Vivica was that Cliff had her first. If that were the case, then he had to question if it was worth it. If Nial slept with Vivica, it would be something on their minds for the rest of their lives as they were connected. He also had a feeling that Vivica and Cliff were far from being over one another. It was rather obvious from the last interaction. Vivica might not have wanted to admit it, but she was clearly still madly in love with the man.

Vivica drove down a street that would take them to the diner. "Oh, look, my bitch of a sister is visiting my mother at home," she said as they passed Gail's house, where apparently Tiffany's car was in the front.

"Do you regret not growing up wealthy even though you had money all around you?" Nial randomly asked.

Vivica made a strange face. "Um... I don't know what you mean. My parents both come from money. My mother just refused to let me spend any of it," she pointed out.

Nial just remembered Margot always discussing Vivica's gold-digging ways. He even would hear his parents on the rare occasion mention how she had a tendency to come off like a gold digger. "Oh... I didn't mean to offend you."

"You've been speaking with your sister, I assume?" Vivica sighed. "Look... I am not going to be rude about it, but there are things I could definitely say about her that make her look a heck of a lot worse than I ever have."

"I don't doubt you. Some of her husbands haven't exactly been outstanding citizens themselves," Nial told her.

Neither have some of the men she just casually saw-like Rodrick Knight. Vivica bit her tongue from revealing this. As much as she hated Margot, she knew that Nial loved her. It wasn't her business to be the one to break it to him or the rest of the Fitzpatrick family. She wished it was, though.

"So, what do you want to do for the rest of the time we have together?" Vivica asked.

Nial looked at her, a little confused. "What do you mean by that?" He didn't want to assume anything with her. Lord knows he had in the past but was too pinheaded to grasp that she wasn't interested.

"Well… I'll be returning to New York after Easter and you back to school," Vivica pointed out.

It was so weird for Vivica to actually want to spend time with him. He was used to her throwing pillows and once a glass at him to get away from her. This almost seemed too easy, which was hard to explain in his mind, but he wasn't going to pass this opportunity up. "Why don't we just go and see where things end up going?"

LANGLEY – JANUARY 2019

This was ridiculous. How could she be the only one who could see exactly what was going on, right in front of all of them? Vivica clearly was orchestrating something against her by getting Amanda Madwell into the same house for the week. Amanda Fucking Madwell. This girl was the real deviant. She slept with anything that moved and was just a brat. Langley was definitely high maintenance, but this girl was just everything you didn't want to deal with. It was beyond her belief that Harry and Brad grew up with this girl, who she had known for only a semester and a half.

The youngest Kingsley child walked into Harry's room,

"She needs to go."

Harry turned around from his desk. "Who needs to go?"

"Amanda Madwell. That girl is trouble. I know what your aunt is up to."

"I think you are being paranoid. Bridget Madwell is an old friend of my aunt's. She owns the agency that aunt Vivica will model for sometimes," Harry tried to defend.

Langley was aware of all of this. It didn't change anything at all for her. Amanda was a different story. That girl could get a priest to undress for her. It was obvious that there was a mutual attraction between Brad and Amanda. Brad might have been a virgin till marriage for any normal girl. It wouldn't be the case for Amanda, which in a way was kind of sick to think that his own mother would sick someone like her onto him.

"Where on earth is Preston?" Langley asked. She knew that Harry might not understand where she is coming from, but Preston would. She and Preston were far enough outside of the Knight-Fitzpatrick worlds but still in it enough to get it.

"I'm not sure where he is, but I'm starting to get worried. I don't want him to be late. That's the last thing he needs to be right now with Aunt Vivica around," Harry said, starting to breathe heavily.

Langley walked over to her best friend and patted him on the back. "Oh, relax, Harry, you know your aunt adores you." She definitely didn't adore Preston. The sad thing is if he was from any other family, it would be a different situation. He was a Costa, though, and Vivica hated the Costa family with a passion of a thousand suns. Vivica tended to hate a lot of people.

MARGOT – JANUARY 2019

"I am not getting myself involved in this drama, Nial. I finally am having things go my way. The house is finally mine and mine alone. I'm in-charge of the company, and the Whore is nowhere around me." She opened the front door. "You better get the heck out and go check yourself into a hotel or something." Margot had put up with her brother for years because of a sense of obligation. The two of them would never say it out loud but were on the verge of middle-age. Margot wasn't about to get herself involved in this nonsense again.

Nial rolled his eyes and walked into the library. He sat down in an armchair. "So, we put up with this favor from Anthony and Jackie, and then I go back to Illinois."

He didn't listen to a damn word she said. "Oh fine... but you better find a new place to stay while here. I am not paying to get blood removed from any inch of this house."

"I'll pay for it if need be," Nial stated. "We just have to play along like usual, and this will be over with soon enough. I'm sure of it," he explained.

This was never going to work, but whatever floated his boat, she guessed. Anthony Costa has had a way of getting things done without getting caught. Nial pretty much gave up on wearing pants a long time ago. He was always caught with them pulled down. What was the use of keeping them on?

"Fine... you can stay here. Don't make me an accessory to any more crimes."

Her younger brother laughed at this. "Oh please, like I haven't helped you cover up much worse things. Let's not forget you were married to a serial killer."

That was the family's go-to blow. Even her own damn son would remind her over and over again that she married a serial killer. She would constantly remind him that the man was his own damn father. Apparently, it didn't matter. "Just promise me you will get this associate of Costa's ready for work and back in the real world soon enough."

Nial shrugged, "I will promise nothing and deliver what I deliver. It's not like I want to be here myself. I'd rather not be around with Vivica and the Knight man getting married."

It was beyond obvious that Nial was still in-love with Vivica. It wasn't a normal love by any means. If it was, he would have kept his pecker in his pants during any one of their three marriages. He might have also considered not divorcing her for a woman that ended up leaving him for a much younger man—a man who mysteriously ended up dead. Margot obviously knew that Nial had paid off Anthony to have one of his men take care of it. She had not been happy. It was her turn to use a kill.

Margot had to put up with Jackie Carson-Costa for six months in a safe house a few years ago to earn that favor. Yet, Nial's dumbass went and used it. "Well then, stay away from them, Nial. It isn't that hard to stay away from your ex-wife of three separate marriages. If I can stay away from my ex-husbands, then you can do the same with your ex."

The blonde brother gave his sister a look of shock. "You cannot compare my marriages to your abominations. You married a serial killer, a man who wanted to extort you and the family, some guy who wanted to be you secretly, and the list goes on…"

"You didn't even get the order right," Margot rolled her eyes. She found herself rolling her eyes a lot when Nial was around. "I have plans at the yacht club this evening." She walked out of the library and grabbed her coat from the front closet.

"Just so you know, I will be going out myself," Nial explained.

His older sister turned around and looked at him. "I do not care. I do not care if you come home at all." She went to open the front door. Margot turned around once more. "Oh… I moved your room down the hall. I needed more clothing storage, so I turned your old room into a closet."

"What happens when mom and dad decide they want to move back in?" Nial asked.

Margot started to chuckle. "Nadia and father are never going to move back. Don't you get it, Nial? We are grown-ass adults at this point. Nadia wants to run around the world, and father will chase her while she does so. It's always been that way."

MARGOT – APRIL 1990

Rochester Hills was new money in the eyes of Margot. She was technically new money, but she had shoved her way into old money society very early in her life. Even still in her eyes, Rochester Hills and the Million Dollar Mile was a step-down from the Fitzpatrick Mansion. Her current house was a modest ten bedrooms with five and a half baths. The pool was an open concept in the backyard, and her neighbors were all stuck-up morons.

At least in Grosse Pointe, people played the game. In Rochester Hills, people purposely chose to stay the fuck out of your sight to avoid having to talk. At first, Margot loved this. It was six months in where things started to get frustrating.

The drive into Detroit could be a dread in the morning, but it was worth it. Fitzpatrick Steel had been flourishing the last couple of years. Margot wanted to invest her time into other projects for the family. They could have owned different ventures like a party planning company, a cosmetic company, and other ridiculous on the surface side businesses that would bring in additional cash flow. Her father had no desire to add on, though.

Her mother had forbidden her from continuing to bring it up. It pissed Margot off to no end that her mother was getting involved. Nadia had never been interested in the company until they moved back home a few years back permanently. All of a sudden, her parents wanted to be one big family unit.

At this point in her life, Margot had just gotten divorced and had one child. She almost immediately got remarried and was pregnant a few years later. She couldn't take her mother being insufferable anymore and chose to move out into her own house.

"Felicia, check on the boys! One of them is clearly crying!" Margot screamed at her nanny as she walked in from the garage entrance.

This new nanny was clearly not going to last. She somewhat suspected that she was sleeping with her husband. That was fine with her. Margot wasn't even sure she loved him at this point. The phone started to ring. Margot reluctantly went to pick it up, "Hello?"

"Hello, Margot. We were wondering what time we should expect you over for Easter?" It was Nadia on the other end.

They had only spoken the night before. She had seen

her father in the office earlier that day. Why on earth was her mother really calling her?

"I suppose later in the day...the boys have to search for the eggs," Margot explained.

"Well, I thought that we could have the easter egg hunt over here. It would be fun to have them hunting around in the backyard. It would be just like when you and Nial were younger," her mother said.

Like when they were younger? "I think you hid eggs for me all of once... Abuelita used to do all of that while you were trying to save the world from flooding or something." Margot had fond memories of Abuelita Lana. She was the definition of a woman who worked hard but also loved her family. Unfortunately, neither her daughter Nadia or granddaughter Margot inherited those traits. They both were hard-working, but neither clearly was great at being a mother.

Margot often asked herself if Nadia even liked being a mother. Even if she did, it was obvious that she preferred being one to Nial over her. Nial got everything, whereas Margot was expected to sit back and smile, normally at her own expense.

Growing up a Fitzpatrick was nothing like the papers seemed to paint it as being. Margot went to Saint Agnes and was raised by her Abuelita while her parents were off playing super spy throughout the other six continents, and she did mean all six of them. They only came back when Nial was born and only stuck around long enough for her to be technically old enough to watch over him. Abuelita had passed away at that point. Margot was sixteen at the time.

She had no desire to watch her younger brother. When it was time for her to go off to college, she had no choice. She found a boarding school for Nial. Her parents were mortified at the thought. Family took care of family. Well, if that were the case, she wanted to know who they had taken care of. It might not have seemed fair. They did take care of both Abuelita and Grandma Ida in their older ages. In the sense that they both lived in the mansion while other people took care of them.

She realized she hadn't spoken in a minute or so... "You know what... We can have it there. I don't need Joshua misplacing eggs all over the property." With that, she hung the phone up.

VIVICA – JANUARY 2019

The table was set. Hannah was already sitting with Lucy, Perry, and Holly. Vivica swore she had invited Holly's husband along for the evening, but he must have been busy with work. The redhead knew that Holly's husband had a lot of resentment towards her. She both understood and didn't at the same time. Vivica paid Holly very well to technically do nothing. She often suspected that he was not fond of the fact that she was probably making more money than he was as a police officer.

"We should be starting in a few minutes," Vivica smiled. Cliff walked in from the hallway entrance of the dining room. Brad and Harry came in with Langley and Preston. She could somewhat handle Preston at this point, but Langley needed to go.

That was where Amanda came in, which incidentally happened only a moment later. The family was finally all there gathered around the table. Vivica sat next to Cliff, who himself was sitting at the head of the table. "It's wonderful for us all to get together," she said. She then looked straight across from her and jumped back in her seat. "Who the hell invited you?"

Mrs. Templeton looked her in the eyes, "The leggy blonde at the other end."

Vivica immediately turned to Langley, "Lawnmower, did you seriously have to ruin this evening?"

Langley choked on her drink, and her eyes widened, "I didn't invite the old bat."

"I wasn't talking about the Whore from Manhattan... I meant the older sister." Mrs. Templeton said matter of fact.

Lucy turned quickly to look at her, "I did no such thing!"

Mrs. Templeton turned and looked back at her, "You certainly did. I remember overhearing you talk about it at my book club."

The redhead rubbed her forehead. "You had book club and didn't invite me?"

Cliff gave her a look, "This is what bothers you about this situation?"

Vivica shrugged, "It's a damn good book club. Just because Mrs. Templeton is a heartless bitch doesn't mean she can't run a good book club."

"That's the nicest thing you have ever said to me," Mrs. Templeton said.

Hannah stood up. "Ok, you old bat... No one invited you! Time to get the hell out!"

"Which twin are you again? Regardless, I don't like either one of you," Mrs. Templeton explained.

Cliff sighed, "You know what... It's not worth trying to kick her out. We will just ignore her."

It was probably for the best, Vivica thought. It wasn't like the entire group hadn't been doing that for years as it was.

"So then... I'd like to announce my bridesmaids." She stood up and looked at the room. "Bridget, of course, you are one of my dearest friends. I'm glad you arrived early so I could ask you in person.

Brianna Belle, who some of you know, will also be a bride's maid. I can't walk down the aisle without the two of you." She then made her way to Hannah and put her hands on her niece's shoulders. "You've always been a daughter more than a niece to me. Will you accept the invitation to stand for your father and me?"

Hannah smiled, "You didn't even have to ask. I've always been your biggest cheerleader."

Vivica then walked across from her and stood next to Lucy. "You were my assistant and almost business partner. I've known you for six years, and I feel like our friendship will last forever. Will you stand for me?"

Lucy got a little teary-eyed, "Of course, Vivica."

The red-haired vixen smiled and went back to her seat.

"Great! I have my bridesmaids!"

Holly got up from her chair, "Excuse me? You asked your damn ex-assistant who used to call you at six AM harassing you to come into the office to be a bridesmaid but not me?"

Vivica turned to Cliff. "See, I told you she would react like this," Vivica turned back to Holly and held both her hands.

"Holly O'Dell, you are the worst maid ever. You also happen to be my best friend. Will you be my maid-of-honor?"

Instead of saying anything, Holly hugged Vivica.

"I'll take that as a yes," Vivica smiled.

Cliff cleared his throat. He looked at Harry, "I understand if you don't want to, but I would love for you to be my best man. You are, after all, the best son a father could ask for."

Harry smiled, "Um... Well... Yes!" Preston kissed him on the cheek. Vivica rolled her eyes.

"When is this wedding so I can remember to be out of town?" Mrs. Templeton asked.

Vivica sighed, "No one said you were invited. Once again, no one invited you tonight!" She screamed at her. It was moments like this that she both loved her life and wanted to bash her head against the wall at the exact same time.

HARRY – JANUARY 2019

Once dinner was over, the teens decided to walk over across the street to his aunt's house to hang out for a little bit. Harry didn't object to it. It would give him some private time with his boyfriend. The two looked into one another's eyes. Preston Costa had the most beautiful brown eyes that Harry had ever laid eyes on.

The two boys had first re-met during the summertime. Preston had just moved home from an Italian boarding school. It had been Langley that had pointed out that Preston clearly had a thing for him. She was right. Langley tended to be right.

Preston touched Harry's chin, "So, are you excited to be your dad's best man?"

"Oh, totally!" Harry said awkwardly, laughing. He was totally excited, but then he thought that a wedding between

Cliff Knight and Vivica Weston meant that everyone on the planet would be there. Plus, what about his mother. They had a falling out once he was outed at the beginning of last year. While the two of them had made up, would it upset her that he was standing in at the wedding? Obviously, Hannah would also be standing, but he knew that Hannah and his mother probably would never have a loving and lasting relationship.

Harry wasn't ready to admit that about his own relationship with their mother. Plus, what if he somehow screwed up and everyone was mad at him.

He started to breathe heavily. Preston rubbed his back,

"Hey, deep breaths. Take long, deep breaths. I'm right here. Nothing bad is going to happen when I'm around you," Preston smiled.

Harry allowed himself to rest his head on Preston's shoulder as they sat in his aunt's living room. Langley then emerged from the kitchen.

"I swear to you, Amanda Madwell is clearly flirting with your cousin. He is definitely enjoying it," She said as she sat down across from them.

"I don't think you have anything to worry about, Langley," Preston said.

The Knight son would agree with that. She had nothing to worry about. Brad was clearly falling-in-love with Langley. It was just that Brad and Amanda had been very close friends in early childhood. He had also been friends with her but not to the same degree. They were like five years old or something. It wasn't like it was some bizarre lifelong crush.

Harry didn't imagine that people could fall for someone that long, especially when it would appear that Amanda clearly had fallen for other people over the years. At least with what Langley was saying about her. He didn't have room to judge. Langley really didn't either, but it was in Langley's nature to do so.

"I think you and Amanda would be better friends than enemies, Langley," he pointed out.

Langley looked at Preston and just started to laugh hysterically, "Oh, how funny." She rolled her eyes.

LUCY – JANUARY 2019

So far, the hotel was running smoothly. If anything, Lucy had run four and five-star hotels with more glitches to them than this place. Raising Langley had more glitches than this place. She had a marvelous office located on the south side of the building. You could see Lake St Clair from a distance. The walls were all red, much like the rest of the hotel itself. She loved the cherry oak flooring that was the original floors. It added something to the building. There was a knock on the door. She hoped it wasn't Margot. She had clearly gone from one neurotic redhead to another. "Come in," said Lucy.

In came a redhead, but they weren't female. "Well, hello, Mr. Fields," Lucy said as she got up from her desk to kiss him. He kissed her back for a full minute, it seemed. "What brings you in today?"

"I just had a little bit of time before my next pitch meeting with the old bat." Perry, of course, meant Mrs. Templeton. Perry had been the only Fitzpatrick to finally get her to sell Templeton ice cream. A profitable ice cream business that someone in the Templeton family had formed back in the late 1800s. There were rumors that it was Mrs. Templeton herself who had done so.

Lucy wasn't sure why Perry would invest so much time into this deal. They both knew that Mrs. Templeton was never going to sell her precious ice cream company. That place was her pride and joy. There were only a few things that woman actually liked in this world, and ice cream, bizarrely, happened to be one of them.

"I can't believe Vivica asked me to be a bridesmaid," Lucy blurted out.

Perry smiled, "I'm sure she won't put you in some hideous-looking dress."

Lucy rolled her eyes, "I wouldn't be so sure about that. She is very much obsessed with being the most attractive woman in the world."

It wasn't a matter of wearing a tacky dress. It had to do with the fact that she had just escaped working for Vivica in the grand scheme of working on parties together. This was essentially getting the old gang back together with her angry niece, airhead model bestie, and the overly cheerful childhood best friend who Vivica admits she thought had a crush on her throughout school. Though she only apparently realized this after discovering that Brianna Belle wasn't into Cliff. Vivica would be high maintenance and freak out about everything, as she always did and always would.

Holly would be a supportive friend and plan the bulk, but Lucy would take on the assistant's role yet again. Then again, this might be the last time that she and Vivica ever worked together. Lucy believed that they would remain friends, but the days of them being at each other's throats over a party were long gone.

Lucy was finally on her own in her career and was proud of herself. She worked so hard to escape this life six years ago when her father was on the verge of getting arrested for his involvement with the Mob. It took a few years, but he finally got caught. He was quietly released several months ago.

Lucy had to make a deal with him to appease him. She would help him get out if he promised to stay out of her life and her younger sister Langley's. She implied he was to stay away from her brother Xander as well, but considering that Xander was now a police officer and there was no doubt that her father Alexander *A-King* Kingsley was back at the old game, he wasn't going to reach out. Langley was a different story. Langley was the child that most celebrated the Kingsley way of life.

The Kingsley's of Manhattan were old money that lost everything during the great depression. It was his father who rebuilt the family name from nothing back in the late eighties. He was a get-rich-quick schemer who happened to crack the code. That code involved getting involved with the Mob. Mind you, they weren't even Italian. He would then fall for their mother, Britney, a sort of model that he met while clubbing back in the nineties. Britney Kingsley had been MIA since Langley was a little girl.

Lucy was given the daunting task of raising her siblings while her mother was *missing,* and her father was acting like a child. She felt bad when she ran for the hills, but she was a grown adult at that point, and nothing was forcing her to stay aside from guilt, which she quickly got over.

Grosse Pointe was supposed to be a meeting. A meeting with Margot Fitzpatrick, who had stayed at a boutique hotel chain that Lucy had helped organize back in Manhattan. She had been impressed with what Lucy had accomplished and told her if she was ever in town to look her up. Lucy did just that, but Margot claimed not to be interested. It was then a chance encounter with a different redhead in the Fitzpatrick Group's lobby that would cement her staying in Grosse Pointe for the past six years.

Vivica offered her way too much money to essentially run her party planning business. It was a huge step down, but it paid the bills rather well. It was during this era she had met Austin Martin, a recent med school graduate who wooed her at the time. They eventually became engaged.

However, shortly after Langley and Xander came to town, it became apparent that Austin had been cheating on her. They broke up, and shortly after, Austin died. She did miss the memory of Austin.

Then, at the end of last summer, she accidentally met

Margot's son Perry Fields. They hit it off right away and ended up falling for each other rather quickly. Margot, soon after, finally offered her this job, and there was no looking back.

Lucy sighed, "I guess it will be one last hurrah before everyone officially starts their new life."

"Oh, I'm sure you will always be connected with Vivica," Perry smiled.

"Considering Langley is off and on with her son and best friends with her nephew, plus Xander is dating her niece, no doubt," Lucy explained. She wasn't sure if any of that was a good thing or not. It was what it was, though.

"I'm more afraid of how this is going to affect Holly. Giving her the task of maid-of-honor is just going to be too much for that girl to handle."

HOLLY – JANUARY 2019

She never intended to work for Vivica for more than a few months. Her husband was on leave from the GPPD, and she needed to get a quick job.

Nadia Fitzpatrick put out an ad in the paper looking for a maid, and Holly swallowed her pride and applied. It was actually Margot who had hired her. However, it was Vivica that she would form a friendship with. The two women definitely did not have a conventional friendship, but there was no doubt that they were best friends.

Holly felt guilty to some degree, taking money for hanging out with her all day long but at the same time being Vivica's friend was a full-time job on its own. Between her constantly running away, coming out of retirement as a model, meddling in her son and nephew's relationships, marrying and divorcing men, and so on, Vivica was a piece of work. A piece of work that she had learned to admire over the years but a piece of work, nonetheless.

Her husband was not a fan of Vivica. He felt that she should either be using her degree or taking care of the children. Their children were of school-age now, though, and knew how to be home for a few hours after school.

Getting the privilege of being Vivica's maid-0f-honor was both a privilege and a big daunting task at the same time. There was no telling how this would inevitably go for any of them.

Even though Holly knew that Vivica loved Cliff with all her heart, it would be up to Holly to make sure that Vivica didn't run for Monaco or one of her two ex-husbands. One of them happened to be Cliff's estranged first cousin, Luke Knight. Holly was up for the task. An actual wedding to the man Vivica had been obsessed with and in love with for years was the end game Holly had been waiting for.

"I just want a simple dress that says stand-out," Vivica said as she looked at the full-length mirror in her bedroom at her old house. The redhead and her maid were currently brainstorming ideas as they packed up the remaining items they were taking with them across the street. Vivica's mansion was purchased by Vivica's second husband and Cliff's cousin Luke. He did it to spite Cliff during an era of time in which the two cousins were not on good terms at all. Things had not changed all that much but being separated by distance made it easier to pretend the other did not exist.

"Well, simple is not a word that fits in your dictionary," Holly said as she flipped through bridal magazines. "You are going to need something that shows people that this is the last time you are going down the aisle."

Holly had never attended any of Vivica's other weddings. Her last wedding to Nial was right before Holly came to work for Vivica. Holly remembered when Vivica divorced Nial the first time. She was rather young at the time and didn't really understand what the big deal was. Nial's son, Rod, had gone to school with her. They really weren't friends, but they weren't enemies either. She just remembers him not reacting very well to the situation. From what she had pieced together about Rod Fitzpatrick, he thought of Vivica as a motherly figure.

Vivica was really a decent mother figure to other people's children. Rod, Hannah, and Harry were all given more time than their actual parents took in being part of their lives. Yet, then you had Laura and Brad. Laura was about six years younger than Holly. She had seen her in passing at Saint Agnes. As far as Holly could remember, Laura was the ultimate Weston-Fitzpatrick hybrid. It must have been some time after she graduated that Laura turned completely against her parents. Holly had no idea what happened with Brad. Brad was like five or six when she came to work for the Fitzpatrick's. Nial shoved him into boarding school as quickly as he possibly could. Vivica was devastated for months during that time. Brad seemed to be happy enough. Tiffany pretty much refused to let Vivica have private time with Harry during this period. Hannah was old enough that she could sneak away after school for a few hours to spend time with her aunt.

Vivica sighed, "I just want this to go perfectly." She looked at Holly, "I've been waiting for this day since I was twelve years old."

"Technically, it happened once," Holly pointed out. That might not have been the best point to bring up.

Her boss gave her a nasty look, "We don't talk about that wedding. Yes, that was a nice period of time, but obviously, it didn't end well."

When Tiffany Knight returned from the dead, Vivica reluctantly allowed her back into Cliff's arms. Holly had no idea why back then, but over the last few years, she had figured it all out. Vivica honestly wasn't the Whore from Beverly Hills that the town had made her out to be. If anything, Vivica's name for Tiffany rang more true than it should have. Tiffany really was a bitch of a sister. She stole Cliff from Vivica once and then demanded that her reality be returned almost exactly from the time she left. It didn't matter that Vivica saved her Hope and Hannah's lives. It didn't matter that she raised the two girls and Harry. Vivica was expected to be given the boot and go back into exile from the Knight family. Holly wanted to believe that Cliff was just trying to do what he thought was best for his family. She honestly had no idea, though. The fact was that Cliff was a laughing stock amongst the not-so-upper elite of Grosse pointe for a long while. The rumor was that the wedding between Vivica and him had been all set to go to the point where Vivica was waiting for him to show up. Only for him to stumble in with Tiffany.

CLIFF – APRIL 1990

"**P**hyliss, you have to eat something!" screamed Delia Knight. Cliff was trying to look over some paperwork before a meeting at Knight. A meeting at Knight... Why was he working at Knight? This was never the plan. The plan was to finish up college and move to wherever Vivica wanted. They would live off her modeling money and wait until the year in which his inheritance would kick in. Then he was going to become a stockbroker. That all went out the window with Tiffany. Tiffany was in med school and wanted to be around her mother, whom she didn't grow up around. Cliff understood that but didn't understand why she insisted on living at North Pointe?

North Pointe held nothing but bad memories for him. The house had changed very little since he was born. Phyliss brought fresh air to the home. Having Sister Mary Newman around also kept his father from completely acting out. Rodrick was always secretly afraid of Sister Mary Newman. Rodrick also liked or at least tolerated Tiffany but always hated Vivica. Rodrick always claimed Vivica was a tramp. Cliff knew the reality; Vivica was one of the few people outside of the family that called him out on his bull shit. She also happened to be connected to the Fitzpatrick family. Technically, Tiffany had the same connection, but she had not grown up around the Fitzpatrick's. DJ Brash, Vivica's step-father, had no part in raising Tiffany.

"Cliff, are we going out tonight?" Tiffany asked. She sat down across from him in the drawing-room.

The Knight heir looked up, "Going out? It's Tuesday. What are we going to go out for?"

Tiffany looked at him as if he was supposed to know the answer to this. "It's my only one night off a week. Didn't you remember?"

Cliff honestly had not. He was thinking about his Weston. Tiffany was still not that Weston. "Well, I mean, I suppose we could go to the diner."

His wife sighed, "You know I hate that place." It was a regular spot of Vivica and his own during high school. "Can we go to the yacht club? We both like the yacht club!" He hated the yacht club, the country club, the more expensive places in Detroit and the suburbs, etc. It was Tiffany who loved all these places. They were not cheap. They obviously had the money, but it was just not his scene at all. He and Vivica had gone

104

to the yacht club for dinner before prom. She laughed at the prices and told him they were going to the diner. Vivica loved wealth and definitely was a poster child, but she was much more down to earth about it. Tiffany wanted to be a Vanity Fair cover model. Which was ironic considering Vivica was the model. Tiffany was the doctor.

Cliff had to question why Tiffany was in med school. She often complained about it to anyone who would listen. His grandmother was starting to roll her eyes when she would talk with Tiffany. It was obvious the only person that was happy about his marriage was his father. It wasn't an approval as much as he was just happy to be rid of Vivica.

"Tiffany, we don't both like the yacht club. You like the yacht club. I can live without having a thirty-dollar sandwich," Cliff blurted out loud.

His wife looked at him in almost terror. "I just thought that we could do something nice! We never do anything nice!" She stormed out of the drawing-room, and he could hear her running up the foyer staircase.

As his wife ran out, his grandmother walked in, "Let her cool off." Delia closed the door. "You know your grandfather was a stone-cold bastard. He lied, cheated, did everything under the sun. I don't condone anything he did, but at least he didn't coddle me."

Cliff felt a little taken back by this comment. "I don't coddle her," Cliff stood up.

Delia chuckled. "Everyone in town sees it, Cliff. I want

what is best for you. This isn't what is best. The redhead is what is best."

"You don't like Vivica," Cliff reminded her as he crossed his arms.

"I don't like that Vivica is so close with the Fitzpatrick family. I think she is a little spacy at times, but I also know she loves you. She has always loved you. When you didn't realize it, the rest of the world did," Delia explained to her grandson.

She sat down. "It's days like this that I wish I still drank. Between your crazy wife and sister, I've just had about enough."

Cliff sighed, "Please tell me you aren't going to start sneaking cigarettes again."

The Latina matriarch laughed, "Oh lord no. I'm going to go pull a double at GPGH. They need all the help they can get right now," she smiled.

"Maybe we can have breakfast tomorrow. Just the two of us like old times," Cliff offered.

His grandmother smiled, "Only if we can go to the yacht club. You know how much we both love the yacht club!" She rolled her eyes and laughed as she walked out of the room.

There were some tough choices that Cliff was going to have to finally make. One thing was becoming more obvious as time went on; his marriage to Tiffany was not a match in heaven. He really wanted to talk with Vivica. The issue at hand was that Vivica had no desire to talk with him, which scared him.

VIVICA – JANUARY 2019

Vivica stormed into Cliff's office at KMC in almost a state of emergency. "Laura is not coming to the wedding! My own daughter will not be at our wedding." She sat on the edge of Cliff's desk.

The Knight CEO looked at his fiancé, "Well, Um, I actually just got some news this morning from Hope."

"Please tell me she RSVP'd," Vivica demanded to hear. She turned and looked at Cliff.

He sighed, "Uh, well, she sends her best, but she really doesn't think it is appropriate for us to marry."

This sunk into her brain for a moment. Her niece that she had a hand in raising, did not seem to want to come to see her own father be happy. Hope lived in the same household that Hannah and Harry had.

Tiffany had always treated her differently than them. It was a bizarre turn of events, but still. She sighed, "Cliff, should we try to get them to come?"

Cliff thought for a moment, "Vivica, at the end of the day, they are both adults at this point. We are too. I think we more than deserve to be happy ourselves. We stayed apart for so long to please everyone else under the sun."

"Well, I know that Laura isn't staying away because she doesn't support our marriage. She just doesn't support me, or her father, for that matter. If anything, us being legally married will be a plus in her eyes." One day she hoped that she would fix her relationship with Laura. It just wasn't going to be today.

"And I know that over time Hope will learn that this is honestly for the best. Tiffany and I were in love at one point. It just hasn't been that way for a long time," Cliff explained.

Vivica remembered that era of time; it wasn't one that she had fond memories of. Yet, at one point, she supposed that she and Nial were also technically in-love. Such a long time ago indeed.

"At least Hannah, Holly, and Bridget all seem to be excited about being bridesmaids," Vivica said.

Her fiancé gave her a strange look, "You forgot Lucy."

"Well, I know she is happy for us and excited about the wedding." Vivica didn't blame her. Lucy had grown out of being Vivica's assistant some time ago.

Vivica was honestly shocked that Lucy had lasted as long as she had. "Eventually, I'm going to have to figure out some sort of a job for myself."

Cliff laughed, "Vivica, how many times do I have to tell you; you don't have to work."

"I need to work, Clifton Knight!" Vivica said, almost annoyed. Even if it was just something part-time, she needed to have a source of income for herself. It was the only thing that made it clear she was not a gold digger. It didn't matter that her savings account had enough in it from her golden days as a supermodel. People still accused her of trying to rob the Knight and Fitzpatrick family's dry.

Cliff looked at her directly in the eyes, "Vivica, the past is in the past. We both know that at no point in your life were you a gold digger."

It was wonderful that Cliff grasped this, but everyone else seemed to think otherwise. Even Nial would constantly accuse her of being one. Yet, it was his idea for them to get married the second time based completely around the idea of them getting a payday from it.

"Hopefully, one-day, things will be completely different. Until that day happens, though, I'm still the Whore from Beverly Hills." She got a text message, "Oh boy…"

"Is it Laura?" Cliff asked, sounding shocked.

Vivica turned and looked at him. "Apparently, Holly won't leave Lucy alone at the hotel. I think I may have to get myself involved."

Cliff nodded, "You should probably take care of that…"

HOLLY – JANUARY 2019

I get a weird vibe from her." Holly met Brianna Belle one time when she had to pick up Vivica from hiding out in California. She had slept on Brianna Belle's couch for a night after she slept with her ex-husband Luke Knight. Luke was Cliff's estranged first cousin. Vivica and Luke had a very messy relationship between her stints with Nial and her illegal marriage to Cliff. Holly got to play the person who fixed everything after Vivica, of course, fucked everything up once again.

Lucy gave Holly a look like she was about to bash her head in. Holly did not appreciate this, "I sort of have to get back to work."

Holly rolled her eyes, "You run a damn hotel! As in run. I was a head maid at the Fitzpatrick mansion and Vivica's house. Did you ever see me lift a finger?"

"I think I saw you make a few sandwiches for yourself," Lucy said with exhaustion in her voice. "I bet you that Bridget Madwell would love to help out. Especially considering she came in early for this. Hannah might want to get involved too!"

The maid sighed, "You just don't get it; Hannah is a bridesmaid because she is her niece. Bridget is a bridesmaid because lord knows why. Brianna Belle..., I don't want to think of the logic there. You and I are the bread and butter that will be holding this together."

The blonde hotel manager took a deep breath as she walked out from behind the front desk's counter. She sat down in the lobby, and Holly followed. Vivica then stormed in, "Oh look, it's Vivica herself now!"

"Good news Holly, we get to go and try on my wedding dress!" Vivica explained. She gave Lucy a wink.

Holly nodded, "Well, that really should be something that is done with all the bridesmaids. Brianna Belle, of course, is not here, so we can omit her."

"It's ready now, though, and I really wanted your final input," Vivica explained to her maid.

The two women went to the showroom out in Rochester Hills. Vivica spent twenty minutes looking at herself in the dressing room mirror.

"Come on, get your ass out here!" Holly screamed, getting anxious.

The door finally opened. "Well, how do I look?" she asked.

It took a full minute for Holly to process how radiant Vivica came off in her wedding dress. Then it hit her, "Really? White again? Vivica, you have been married four times with an illegal ceremony thrown in for good caution. Do you really think it makes sense to wear white again?"

The redhead gave her a dirty look. "I was married three times to the same man. White is traditional. That concept went out the door a hundred or so years ago and was only upheld for so long because of "anti-women's" women groups starting in the '50s. On top of that, I didn't wear white to my first wedding, I wore my jeans. At my second wedding, I was in a blue dress at city hall, and at my third wedding, I wore jeans again. At the fake wedding with Cliff, I did wear white. Then my fourth marriage, well, I burned that dress with you last year if you remember correctly."

Oh, she remembered burning the dress. Holly had to get her husband to drop the charges from the city on how much smoke she caused in her backyard. Mrs. Templeton and her sister Tiffany had both called the police on top of a handful of neighbors. Still, it was a fun night. If only Lucy hadn't been bitching the entire time about them having real work to do. Lucy was a rather big killjoy to the fun.

"Well, ok then, Vivica. You can wear white," Holly wasn't going to argue when Vivica was clearly on a roll.

The two continued to look in the mirror as a familiar

blonde man's reflection caught their eye. He was walking outside. Vivica turned to Holly. Holly rubbed her forehead. This was the last thing they needed today.

VIVICA – JANUARY 2019

It was as if the world had decided to play a cruel trick on her. She did not need this. She gave Holly her purse, "If a sales associate asks where I went, give them my credit card."

Things were finally going the way that they were supposed to. It had taken several decades, but this was the life that Vivica was meant to live. She wasn't about to let... "Nial Fitzpatrick! What the hell are you doing here?" she asked, as she dragged the expensive wedding dress across the sidewalk of downtown Rochester Hills.

The doctor turned around, a little shocked to see her.

"Viv? What are you doing here?" He clearly looked her up and down. "I see you are preparing for your foolish wedding to the Knight loser."

"You didn't answer my question. Why are you here?" Vivica asked, annoyed.

Nial sighed, "I knew I would run into you sooner or later. Honestly, I didn't expect it to be in a different county of all places. I'm just home temporarily to help out a friend of mine."

"Nial, you have no friends," Vivica thought about it for a moment. "Oh, for crying out loud, please tell me you aren't helping Costa out. Nial, you idiot!" Vivica screamed at him.

"You know for as much as you and Margot hate one another, you often sound a lot alike." Nial gave her a dirty look,

"I'm just helping him with a medical situation."

Vivica knew damn well that Anthony Costa wasn't sick. A medical situation meant that the Costa organization fucked up and needed help with something illegal. "You better keep Brad far from this situation," as she thought about Harry dating Preston. "And Harry, for that matter, does Preston Costa know you are home?"

Nial looked at her, confused, "How the heck would I know? Costa and Jackie come over to the house. I don't go over there."

She took solace in knowing that this meant that Margot was roped into this situation. "Nial... I'm getting married to Cliff."

"Yes, Viv. I can clearly see that...," he pointed to her dress.

"I need you far away from Cliff and me. Nothing is going to stop us from getting married this time," Vivica crossed her arms.

Her ex-husband nodded his head, "I'm just going to point out that at no point did I ever keep you from Cliff. I don't really have a desire to get back with you. Do you have a desire to get back with me?"

Vivica started to laugh, "I'd rather clean Mrs. Templeton's toilets for a year." Then she sighed, "Look, just stay away from North Pointe and the wedding. Maybe spend some time with your damn son, though. I know it is a crazy concept!" She rolled her eyes and stormed back into the dress shop. She looked at Holly, "I don't want to hear it."

The maid sat down in an armchair. "Well, they charged you for the dress," as she handed Vivica the bill.

"Why on earth is this three hundred more than the catalogue said?" Vivica asked.

"I bought shoes," Holly whispered.

Vivica looked down, "Those are some damn nice shoes."

LANGLEY – JANUARY 2019

Harry and Brad were sitting together with Amanda as if they were old friends. They were old friends. Amanda was all over both boys. Obviously, Harry was gay. Brad wasn't, though, and Brad didn't even let her hang all over him. Yet, Amanda could? Amanda, who slept with their damn teacher, could do this, but she couldn't. Langley turned to Preston, who was sitting next to her in the park, "You grew up with the girl too, right?"

"Well, not in the same way as Harry and Brad. I never really hung out with them until I started going out with Harry. I mean, I was away at boarding school for several years, but even so," Preston explained to her.

Langley knew that Brad had many issues with Preston and his family. Brad had spent several months as a Preston, living with Anthony as a baby. Jackie had fled town with the real Preston, and Nial lied to Vivica, claiming that Brad had died at birth and gave Brad to Anthony to keep him from going off on him. Jackie eventually returned to town with the real Preston in hand. Brad grew up with a strong distaste for the Costa family because of this.

Harry being anti-social, just did what his cousin did. This was something that she admitted drove her crazy about the cousins. Brad would have strong opinions on something, and Harry would just automatically agree with it even when it was more than obvious that Harry didn't agree.

"So, was she just as slutty back then?" Langley demanded an answer.

Preston gave her a look, "I don't think so. We were all under ten. I mean, anything is possible. The three of them were definitely inseparable until Brad went off to boarding school and Amanda moved to New York."

What made no sense is the fact that Amanda lived in Grosse Pointe, to begin with. Her mother was a big-time New York-based model. This town and its history never made any sense to Langley. The blonde really did vie for the days of Manhattan. New York and big city life made sense to her. Grosse Pointe might have been wealth, but it was suburban wealth, in the same way that Long Island was suburban wealth.

Aside from those who summered in the Hamptons and lived in the city, people were not usually cut from the same cloth. Yet, this was her life now. She was a part of the suburban

Midwest. A trip to the country club was considered a luxury. A day out in West Bloomfield or Rochester Hills was considered a day out, but Detroit was not New York City.

It was definitely more thriving than the rest of the country gave it credit for. It just wasn't thriving in the same way that New York or Chicago were. There were definitely things to do down there, but there wasn't a fashion district, there wasn't a thriving theatre district, and most of the nightlife existed slightly outside the city reach.

It wasn't lost on Langley by any stretch of the means that this was the first time in her life that she had a set friend group. The Kingsley girl had many friends out in Manhattan. They just weren't people she was close to. Had they been her friends? Definitely not in the way that she was friends with Harry and Preston. Her boyfriends were sex partners. Brad was a confidant and very judgmental but well-meaning, nonetheless.

"You shouldn't worry about Amanda. Brad isn't the type to stray. You know that," Preston reminded her.

No, Brad was not. It wasn't Brad that she was worried about. Amanda's sexual exploits were more legendary than her own. This was a girl who had been kicked out of every boarding and day school on the East Coast for crying out loud. Saint Agnes was just another check box for her.

Langley wasn't about to let this tramp use Brad for his penis and then move on to the next penis in a new town. "I will try my hardest," Langley sighed.

NIAL – APRIL 1990

"Well, spill it, little brother. Where have you been spending all your time since you have been home?" Margot asked Nial.

"Oh, just here and there." Nial knew better than to admit to spending time with Viv. The two women couldn't stand one another. It also didn't help that he was technically related to Vivica. It was through marriage, though, and his uncle had long passed on. It was morbid to think about it like that. He couldn't help but try to think of a universe where things worked out with Viv. She was so beautiful. She also had more of a brain than he expected her to have. Sure, she seemed difficult, but between his mother and sister, he was used to difficult women. It made sense that he would be attracted to one. "I'm just spending time with some old friends."

Margot poured herself a cup of tea. The two sat in her kitchen. She rolled her eyes. "Sure, you are… How many friends of yours lack a cock?"

Always blunt and vulgar. That was his sister in a nutshell.

"I mean, I'm not getting laid if that's what you are implying, my dear sister," Nial smiled. It was true. He hadn't slept with Viv yet. He deeply wanted too though. The concept of seeing her naked turned him on greatly. He actually needed to get it off his mind now. The blonde looked back up at his sister, who was giving him a look of disbelief.

"I really am not with anyone right now," said Nial.

"Oh, kid… I raised you. I know you too damn well. Let's not act like you can put anything past me," Margot smiled.

He hated that his sister knew him so damn well. Few people did, but it was true. She did raise him. Their parents had been off playing spy for the bulk of his childhood.

"I mean, look, there might be someone, but it hasn't gotten past a few kisses," Nial admitted.

Margot gave him a look of approval. "Well, good for you. If she is a keeper, then keep her. If she isn't, then use her without abusing her and move to the next one. That's how I've always treated men."

Nial realized that his sister and he had an odd relationship. They would talk very openly about their sex lives and their conquests. Margot always seemed to be more business-oriented though than sex-driven, whereas Nial did everything to seal the deal. Even med school was just a chance to get more women to take their top off for him. People loved the concept of a doctor. They loved it, even more, when they learned his last name was Fitzpatrick. It meant that he wasn't going to be spending the next thirty years paying off student loans. The name might not have had the same ring as Knight but fuck the Knight name.

"What do you think of the Knight family? Really," as he looked at his sister in the eye.

Margot gave him a curious look. "They really don't bother me in the way that they piss off our parents. If anything, our parents overplay the obsession. That said, the entire Knight family does the exact same thing. It's a family feud based around a bad sale that the Knight family concocted, and the Fitzpatrick family stopped. Is it our fault that our aunt and Delia Knight set things in our favor two generations later? Fuck no."

"You knew Aunt Susan, right?" Nial asked. He had never really heard her name brought up around the household. It was almost as if she didn't exist until you looked through old photo albums.

The red-haired Fitzpatrick sighed, "I was maybe a year or so old when she passed away. I don't know. You are better off asking that nun about her than myself," Margot explained.

The nun. Nial couldn't help but laugh, "Why do you hate Sister Mary Newman so much?"

This seemed to be a trigger for Margot as she gave him an evil look. "I don't hate her brother. I just feel that she gets involved in things that aren't her business. Such as the original sin that ignited the Knight-Fitzpatrick feud."

He himself had only attended Saint Agnes for a few years before being shipped off to boarding school. Sister Mary Newman seemed like a typical nun. Overly strict but would smile when it suited her.

"I suppose that is true. So, then, are you coming to dinner tomorrow?" Nial asked.

"I have some sort of playdate planned for Joshua," Margot flat out said.

"Rather convenient," Nial laughed.

His sister smirked, "Don't let my refusal to get involved in family affairs stop you from enjoying yourself," as she rolled her eyes.

Nial continued to laugh, "Oh yes... I love watching dad act like a family man about ten years too late while mom looks like she would rather be polishing her guns and knives."

It had been after the death of her brother and their uncle DJ that made Nadia and Brandon move back to town. At first, they were still wandering around the world off and on, and then all of a sudden, they decided to make their move home permanent.

After years of letting others run the family business, Brandon was finally in charge. It was also the least profitable the company had ever been. Margot made sure that the entire family knew this. Nial knew in his heart of hearts that his sister should be running the company.

MARGOT – JANUARY 2019

The red-haired CEO flung open her front door and then slammed it. No one appeared, so she slammed it again. It took a moment, but her son Perry walked in from the other room. "What's wrong, mother?" he asked.

"Don't act so unconcerned. This affects your inheritance as much as mine," she explained. She stomped her foot on the ground. "Damn it! Our stock fell five points today."

Perry gave his mother a look of disbelief, "Oh, how will we ever recover? I'm going out for the night with Lucy."

All of a sudden, Nial walked downstairs covered in blood. He looked at Perry, "I didn't realize you were home."

His nephew seemed unphased, "So, yeah, I'm going to take out…" He walked towards the back hall where the garage door was.

"You better not have gotten my floors dirty," Margot screamed at him. "Why on earth is there so much blood?"

"I have no idea. This mother fucker just won't heal!" Nial explained.

The Fitzpatrick daughter did not want to deal with her brother's incompetence. "Just promise me you will use old pictures of the Whore from Beverly Hills to clean up."

Nial laughed, "It's funny. I ran into her today."

This intrigued Margot. "How much of a freak out did she have about seeing you?"

"Not as big as you would probably expect, to be honest," Nial admitted.

This annoyed Margot. She wanted Vivica to be pissed off. At the same time, she really didn't want Vivica to even know that Nial had been in town. The last thing she really wanted for her idiot brother's Whore of an ex to be getting the idea of rekindling her romance with him. Every damn time they were in the same room together, some sort of fucked up sparks would start to flare up. They were not a stable couple.

She was about to say something when the doorbell rang.

"Well, are you going to get that?"

"I'm sort of covered in blood," he said as he ran back upstairs.

"Why is it so hard to get someone else to answer the damn door in this household?" Margot asked as she opened the door. It was her nephew, "Oh, it's you... Um, Brian."

"Brad, why do you always forget my name?"

She shrugged. It had nothing to do with the fact that Nial had been drunk when he filed the birth certificate and wrote down Bradly instead of Brandon.

"It's been a long day. What can I do for you? No, let me guess, you've had enough of your mother, and you want to come to live here? I'll allow it."

Her nephew rolled his eyes, "That's not the case at all. My mother happened to tell me that my father was back in town. I was just wondering why he hasn't found the time to tell me this."

That was actually a good question. "Well, he is around here somewhere. You can come in," she said. Then she looked at him. If he didn't have the Vivica in him, he would be the perfect Fitzpatrick.

"You know, you can come over whenever you want," Margot said.

Joshua was a crazy bohemian, and Perry was snippy. Rod, Nial's first son, was hiding from Nial. Laura, Nial's daughter, was hiding from the Fitzpatrick name itself. Brad was the family's last hope at continuing on the legacy of the Fitzpatrick name for what Margot had made it stand for over the years. This was something that she had to give the Knight family credit for. They didn't abandon their family legacy. The Fitzpatrick's had been trying to since they gained it.

Nial awkwardly walked back downstairs in a bathrobe.

"Son! It's so good to see you!" he said, taken back by the fact that his son was home. Brad walked right up to him and punched him in the stomach. "I see your mother has been speaking with you."

"Stay away from mom and Cliff's wedding," Brad said. He turned around stormed out the front door.

CLIFF – APRIL 1990

"So, then your day has been going well?" Cliff asked Tiffany. They, of course, were at the Club. He hated the Club. She insisted upon it, though, instead of staying home or going to the Arbor Inn. Cliff could hear Mrs. Templeton screaming at a bartender, and he swore that he saw his father walk in and out with at least two other women in the last hour. This evening was dreading on.

He remembered the few times that he had taken Vivica to the Club. She clearly enjoyed it more than she let on, but she made it fun. In high school, Vivica was always able to find liquor or get the music changed to be something good.

Tiffany wanted to put on an act that they were Knight's. Tiffany didn't hesitate to take the Knight name. Vivica explained that she would take his name but that she would probably still go by the Weston name publicly for her brand. Cliff had no issue with that. He had no issue with the fact that Tiffany had wanted his name. It was normal, and yet she wore that name like a status symbol.

His wife smiled, "It's been a fantastic day so far. I can't wait to get back to the hospital tonight, though."

She was going back to work. Cliff wanted to groan but stopped himself. Tiffany had been working extra hours for the last month and a half. She was insistent that it was to get her name up there within the hospital.

Cliff honestly wondered if she really wanted to be a doctor to help people or because she liked the concept of being called a doctor sometime. He had seen her around patients briefly. It didn't seem like she enjoyed herself at all. "Do you know who I heard was trying to enroll into the summer program?"

"I have no idea," Cliff said. Why on earth would he know?

Tiffany's smile lit up, but it was in a way that she had some good gossip to share. Cliff didn't care for gossip at all.

"Ok, so I heard that Nial Fitzpatrick would be back in town after the end of this semester for the summer. He is looking to get into the summer program. I have it on good authority that he will not be getting in, though, as we need to keep the Fitzpatrick's out of the hospital, obviously."

Cliff winced at her, "You realize that your mother and sister consider themselves Fitzpatrick's, right? Your step-father was Nadia's brother."

She shrugged, "I wasn't even at the wedding. My mother and I would talk on the phone once a week. It's great that I am getting the chance to spend time with her now. It doesn't mean I agree with her concept of being involved with the Fitzpatrick's. They are trash."

It wasn't that he had much use for Margot, and Nial was obviously becoming a rather sore subject. Nadia and Brandon, however, had never been anything but nice when he was around them. The most conflict that had come from them was after he and Vivica had broken up. It was clear they took her side. Understandable. Tiffany was only going by what his father, and father alone said about them. "You know my grandmother was dear friends with the late Susan Fitzpatrick. Sister Mary Newman was as well and is also a friend to the Fitzpatrick's."

"Rodrick and I were talking about that. It seems like a rather bizarre thing to have someone with such connection living at the house helping raise his child."

Tiffany took a sip of her drink and looked at herself in a little compact that she had in her purse. "When we have children, I don't want someone with any conflict attached raising them. Obviously, we are going to find the best nanny in town."

Yet again, Cliff was left raising an eyebrow to his own wife, "Tiffany, I didn't even have a nanny…"

This seemed to catch her off guard, "Well, you had the butlers and maids plus your grandparents. Obviously, Rodrick was a very busy man."

Cliff had never really thought about it, but he realized now that Tiffany had never really been given the lowdown on his relationship with his father. Even Cliff had to acknowledge that his father treated Tiffany about a thousand times better than he ever did Vivica, which made no sense. These two women were blood sisters! When he thought about it, though, it made his blood turn cold. He left the love of his life for her sister. Yes, they were technically separated, but that was not the first time.

Vivica was an over-the-top individual that could definitely frustrate him. However, they just worked together. They really did.

He was able to give her realism while she made him venture out of his comfort zone. That was why they were both ready to leave town together after their wedding. He still had a month left on the lease for the apartment in New York, which was not even stepped in since they picked it out together.

"We should have dinner with your father soon. I'd like to get his input on a few things!" Tiffany said this without explanation as to what.

This conversation was eye-opening and obviously the last straw. "I'm leaving... I'm sorry. Actually, I don't know if I am sorry," as he got up and didn't wait for a response from his wife. His wife...

BRAD – JANUARY 2019

"Ok, I got you some ice and pain pills," Langley explained as she sat down next to him on his bed. It was weird how different his room's layout was in the Knight house as opposed to his mom's mansion across the street. He was still getting used to it, adding to the overall pain he was feeling.

He kissed her on the forehead, "Thanks." Brad felt like an idiot punching his own father. "You and your father had a good relationship, right?"

His girlfriend pondered the subject for a moment. "I mean, it kind of blindsided me when he called from jail to tell me about it... I didn't hate him as Lucy does, though. I think Xander was always neutral towards him. You could obviously tell that he was turning out to be more like A-King than he wanted to be, which is why I think he joined the police academy. The issue is that his problems didn't align with those morals. It was with cheating on women. I don't think being an officer of the law would help with that."

This conversation maybe wasn't helping. It seemed as if he was doing the identical thing with his father and maybe even his mother. "I guess for me, it's just difficult to separate the parents that I know from the figures the public know." He knew his parents loved him. Well, he knew his mother loved him. Nial was a different situation. Did he love him because he really wanted to or because he was his son? On top of that, was there resentment because he had Weston blood in his veins?

"Honestly, my relationship with my father was different. He let me do what I wanted, and I let him do what he wanted. There were definitely more than a few occasions where it was hard to tell who was throwing the rave at our penthouse," Langley frowned. Brad could tell she wanted to be of more help with his dilemma but couldn't be. Langley embraced her wealth and upbringing, whereas Brad tried his hardest to run from it.

"I know I come off as being a certain way. What you have to understand is that I don't know how to embrace my parents and their choices," Brad explained. He looked at his girlfriend and really looked at her for once. She was beautiful; breathtakingly so. He leaned in to kiss her again but this time on the lips. She kissed him back and started to put her hand on his thigh. Normally he would stop her from doing this, but this time he didn't stop. She started to get deeper into his thigh, though, and it made him twitch. He stopped and looked her in the eye. Brad could read what she was thinking by just looking into her beautiful grey-blue eyes. He nodded as to tell her she can continue. Langley started to move her hand towards his crotch. Once again, he flinched, but he didn't stop her. It felt good. He had never had another person touch him in this way.

Brad didn't want to be his parents. There were so many thoughts running through his head. He could let this continue, and it would feel good, or he could stop this. If he did, though, Langley might finally lose it.

Before he could say anything, she was unzipping his pants. Brad's normal reaction would be to stop, but for whatever reason, at this moment, he started to take her top off, followed by his own shirt. Langley started to kiss him again, but this time on the neck. She started to move her way down to his chest, kissing and then maybe even licking his nipple. They were getting hard, and that wasn't the only thing that was starting to become hard. Who was he kidding? That had been rock hard for a while. Langley made her way to her knees. She looked up at him. "Last chance to stop," she explained. Brad nodded. He wanted this. He wanted to not be responsible for once, and he wanted to do it in the most pleasurable way possible. He bent up in order to pull down his jeans and then briefs. His cock whipped, and Langley starred at it in what looked to be pure bliss.

VIVICA – APRIL 1990

Why was it that her mother only chose to run out for a quick second on nights where she was wearing a full mask and curlers? Vivica reluctantly walked down the Weston-Brash family staircase. "Just one second," she said unenthusiastically. Instead of doing the smart thing and looking through the peephole, she just blindly opened the door. "What the hell are you doing here?" Vivica asked as Cliff stood there looking out of breath.

"Can I please come in?" he asked her.

Could he come in? For what? Did he want to ask about something that might help please his bitch of a wife? "I'm sort of busy, and my mother isn't home to enable your sham of a marriage."

She went to close the door, but he stopped her. "That's

fine. I need to talk with you and only you. Please, Weston."

It was only upon him calling her Weston that she was able to give in. It felt like good old times for some reason, even though she knew those were dead in the water. She gestured for him to come in.

"Well, what do you want?" she asked.

Cliff grabbed her hands, "I need you to forgive me." She smacked him across the face.

"Ok, I deserved that." She smacked him again. "I probably deserved that too." Vivica was about to smack him again, but he stopped her. "Look, I'm sure I deserved what you have to dish out, but can you please just hear me out?"

Hear him out? She started laughing. "We were going to reschedule the damn wedding. We had a misunderstanding. A minor one in comparison to some of the nonsense we have been through together over the years. I had to go to Europe for one week. One week Cliff! I would have been back in time for the damn wedding. Instead, I come home to find you and my long-lost bitch of a sister kissing in bed together!"

Vivica marched over to the couch and sat down in a huff. "I don't have time to listen about how you still want to be friends. I've moved on as much as I can. I hope you enjoy your purgatory between this earth and the next in Grosse Pointe for the rest of your life. I'll have to move on."

Cliff walked over to the couch and sat next to her, "You don't understand. I want to be with you. I should never have left you for Tiffany."

"Oh, now you see to grasp that. Well, no shit Clifton Knight! You married a woman you knew nothing about, and to add insult to injury, she is my bitch of a sister! This town calls me the Whore from Beverly Hills, and yet that bitch lives with you."

"I'm realizing now that maybe I don't have anything in common with Tiffany," Cliff admitted.

This was rich. He had nothing in common with someone he had only known a few months, who was also several years older.

"Well, you might want to alert the press on that one! The idiot man child isn't sure he has anything in common with his bride he knew nothing about! What are you going to tell me next; the sex was awkward as hell the first time around? Well, hopefully, your dick of a father and his mistress didn't walk in on the two of you as they did with us!"

She wasn't about to let him try and backtrack the months of betrayal. How was Cliff able to come over to her house and act like this was a simple mistake? It wasn't. It was just the icing on the cake. "You wanted us to be friends. My mother wanted us to all get along. She has an excuse because the bitch of a sister is her child as well. You're apparently just braindead. I should have listened to the Fitzpatrick's…" Vivica screamed at him.

The Knight man frowned, "I deserve all of this. I deserve more."

This was Cliff Knight. The man that she had fallen head over heels in love with the moment she laid eyes on him. He was a beautiful creature of a human being. His eyes were perfect. He had an evil Knight smile which just made him look even sexier. "I can't look at you," Vivica said.

"I'm sorry. I know I screwed up," Cliff almost sobbed.

Vivica turned away from him. "I can't look at you because you make me want to forgive you with your gorgeous face. I won't do it anymore. You need to leave!"

"What if I left her Weston? The plan was to leave Grosse Pointe. We could leave and never look back at this mess."

Could she even do that at this point? Could she just pretend that this mess never happened? That was the question.

LANGLEY – JANUARY 2019

This just happened. This just fucking happened. Langley laid her head on Brad's chest. His heart was pounding like a drum. She smiled. "Calm down there," the blonde girl giggled.

"I can't help it. We just did that. I can't believe we just did that," Brad said.

He had the *I just lost my virginity* smile on his face. She had seen that face many a time over the years. It was maybe going to be the last time she ever would. This was the first time in her life that she ever thought that this could be the boy she spent the rest of her life with. That had never been a concept for her in the past. It was always about the conquest until she or the boy would get bored of one another. Then she would move on to the next.

Brad was different. Brad made her work for his compassion but not in a mean way. In a way that made her want to be better and showed him that she was. This was an earned victory. Was it the best lay of her life? No. Was it the most important? Probably.

"Harry is going to flip out when I tell him," as she sat up in bed next to him.

Brad turned to her, looking mortified. "Langley! You can't tell people about this."

"Ok, fine. You can tell Harry first," Langley laughed. She didn't care.

Her boyfriend continued to look mortified. "This isn't something that we need to share with people. This is something special between the two of us."

This was the Brad she knew, a real drip. She sighed,

"I suppose we can keep it to ourselves for now. However, eventually, we are going to have to admit something. People are going to start questioning why you are a thirty-year-old virgin." She thought about this for a second. "Brad, do you have regrets about what we just did?"

He looked at her and started to frown, "I don't have any regrets. I have a million thoughts going through my head right now. I just always thought I would be waiting until marriage."

"We aren't living in the 1950s. People have sex, and they aren't afraid to hide that they do."

Langley never understood why Middle America was so afraid of the word sex when they were clearly all having it. Those teen moms weren't all from the coasts. If you added the ages of the children of many parents to their children, many of those parents were only eighteen at the time of their birth.

"We clearly still need to loosen you up!" she smiled.

Brad gave her a dirty look, "I don't know if I can change overnight, Langley."

She gave him a kiss, "That's fine. I don't expect you to change at all. One of us needs to be practical. However, one of us needs to be able to party. That's where Vivica and Nial stop working as a couple. They are too much alike internally. That's why Vivica works better with Cliff. He's the practical one while she can be a little crazy. It works for them better."

Even if she hated Brad's mother, Brad didn't need to hear that, considering his mother had no issue with giving everyone under the sun her opinion of her. "Let's just enjoy the moment, and then reality can come back. How does that sound?" Brad nodded.

VIVICA – JANUARY 2019

"It's nice that we are finally able to sit down and catch up alone!" Vivica explained to Bridget Madwell as they sat in her mansion. She was still unsure of what she was going to do with the home. It was bizarre to own a home right across the street from where she now lived.

"You definitely seem to be a very busy person even though... well, you aren't modeling anymore," Bridget said point-blank.

This sounded odd to hear. She wasn't modeling anymore. The name Vivica Weston used to be in the headlines. She was on the cover of magazines far before much of the trash of Hollywood was on them. Yet now, she was a Grosse Pointe housewife. "I mean, I did do that tribute shoot last year!"

Bridget nodded, "It sold rather well. You know I

constantly get calls and emails asking to use you for different projects."

It wasn't that Vivica didn't want to be a model anymore. It was that she was needed in Grosse Pointe for Cliff's sake. This was where he worked. Their children were here. Brad and Harry still had another year to go to school. She had already lost so much time with Brad between boarding school and running away from Cliff last year alone. "I mean, maybe once Brad graduates."

"I wish that I had the same relationship with Amanda that you have with Brad," Bridget explained.

She wished she had the same relationship with Brad that Bridget seemed to be alluding to. "I mean, Brad and I definitely have a close enough relationship, I suppose."

It could have been closer, but she lost out on the chance of raising him during his early teen years, which might have been a blessing or a curse. She remembered how difficult Laura had been going through puberty. At least she was female and knew what to expect. Brad would have been a different story.

"I think having Amanda at Saint Agnes will definitely help out in getting her underway, which is what I wanted to talk with you about. Obviously, I can't commute back and forth between here and the coasts plus the other side of the world. Do you think that Cliff would mind if Amanda stayed here with you? She wouldn't even have to stay here. I could get her an apartment. I just would love it if you could check up on her from time to time," Bridget explained.

This was no problem for the redhead. Her husband would be more difficult to convince, as he wasn't the biggest Bridget fan. It was the 90's. They all had different mindsets back then, when she was married to Nial. Bridget might have been dating someone that Cliff didn't approve of, but again, it was a different time. "I suppose I can ask him about it. I'd love for Brad and Amanda to be close again. They seem to be bonding."

"Now, Vivica, are you trying to hook up your son with my daughter?" Bridget asked with a keen smile on her face.

That was exactly what she was trying to do. It didn't even have to be a permanent thing. She just knew that anyone was a better match for her son than Langley Kingsley. That girl would break her son's heart. She knew this because once upon a time, she was Langley. Brad needed someone on a different level. "Is it so wrong to want the best for my child?"

Bridget played with her hair, "I have an idea that wouldn't involve an arranged relationship."

"Do tell," Vivica said as she took a sip of her drink.

"As much as you hate the girl, Langley has a look that I have to say I love. I wouldn't mind signing her for this new project that I have. It would take her away from Grosse Pointe. She would have to live on the West Coast at least for the next year," Bridget explained.

This was the best idea that Vivica had heard all day. All week even. "I think I love the idea. There is no way she will go along with it. The girl genuinely likes Brad and is friends with

Harry. She isn't going to just leave. Plus, there is also Lucy, her sister. There is no doubt in my mind she would disapprove."

The modeling agent shrugged, "She could always ask her father then."

Vivica laughed, "Her father is in jail."

This seemed to cause Bridget to give her an odd look. "In jail? Clearly, you don't keep up with the trades. No, Alexander Kingsley was released months ago. It was sort of brushed under, but he is out," said Bridget.

Well then, Alexander Kingsley was out of prison. This was information that Vivica could play with. "I think my plan has reached new horizons in general. I need to get going," Vivica explained. She got up and grabbed her purse. "Feel free to stick around. I have to go and speak to a hotel manager."

HARRY – JANUARY 2019

"Preston, do you mind if I ask you a question," he asked as he took a lick of an ice cream cone in the school cafeteria.

His boyfriend nodded, "Sure! What's up?"

"Did you know that my uncle Nial was back in town?" Harry asked. He didn't want to come off as accusatory, but he knew that Nial was very good friends with the Costa family.

The Mobster's son looked a bit confused. "Harry, I don't really pay attention to things that involve my parents unless they get me involved. Plus, I have to admit, I'm not much bigger a fan of Nial Fitzpatrick than Brad is of my family. It's not because of the stuff that happened when we were babies, but pretty much about everything that has happened since then."

Harry knew that a lot of people were not fond of Nial. He was always indifferent. It always seemed that the family feud was let go in terms of himself and his sisters, at least with Nial, potentially because of his aunt's blood relationship.

Even though Nial was no longer married to his aunt, he still considered him an uncle figure. At least more than he considered Luke to be his uncle, but Luke was also his cousin. It could get confusing as to who was related to who in this town sometimes.

"I mean, I believe you. Honestly, I assume you would have told me," Harry said.

Preston took a deep breath, "I would have told you if it was important, but if it was something that had to do with my parents' business life, though, I might not. Unless I thought it could affect myself, in which case it might affect you as well. If that makes any sense."

Normally this would be when Harry would start to overthink, but he trusted Preston. "Have you seen Langley today?"

"No. Why?" Preston asked his boyfriend.

"She was acting bizarre this morning. It was almost like… well, I don't know how to describe it. Less overwhelmed about something. Then I spotted Brad coming out of confession before lunch. It was a bit weird. I'm not going to say anything to him, though."

Harry knew that Brad was not happy about his father

being home. Langley had come over the night before in order to help calm him down at Harry's request. He didn't see either of them for the rest of the evening. Which was odd because he had been downstairs in the dining room studying. He was shocked that he hadn't seen Langley slip out. However, she might have used the back entrance. It probably was the case since his aunt had been in the Drawing Room for most of the evening, and he knew that Langley had no desire to be around her.

Preston started to laugh, "I'm sorry, I just... only your cousin would go to confession on a school day. What could he have possibly done? Swear one too many times?"

Harry couldn't say that he didn't see where Preston was coming from with this. Brad was known for being a little too Catholic sometimes. It wasn't that Harry himself wasn't also. It was just that Brad could take things to the next level. "Are you religious?" he asked his boyfriend.

The straight-haired boy pondered for a second, "Yes and no. I believe that there is a higher power and that there is an afterlife of some sort. I just don't know if I believe the bible to be an accurate portrayal of being a good person. I think that people should just be good people, especially when they choose to highlight in a long sentence excuses to hate the two of us but then ignore every other part. I mean, look at Mrs. Templeton," Preston pointed out.

He did make good points. Harry couldn't deny that. Mrs. Templeton might have been an extreme but effective example, though. "I've always believed in God. I guess I've never really thought much into the actual teachings of Catholicism."

"Anything in moderation is fine. It's when you overdo it that it becomes an issue. Obviously, yes, we go to Catholic school. That's more because of our upbringing and privilege than anything else," Preston pointed out.

That was true. He imagined that he would go to a non-religious school if he lived in a different part of the state. Harry remembered begging his parents to let him go to the same boarding school that Brad had gone to. His father, Cliff, was adamant that he was not leaving. His mother had a different view. When his aunt found out that his mother was ok with this, she went nuts.

In all reality, there was no chance that Harry would have been able to get through boarding school, even with Brad.

VIVICA – APRIL 1990

"We would have to leave Grosse Pointe forever. My mother would pretty much disown me, and your family probably won't be fond of the situation. I don't have the nerve to deal with people calling me a Whore and slut and now homewrecker," Vivica explained to Cliff. This was also something that was going through her own head. She was actually putting thought into running away with Cliff. This shouldn't have been a shock to her. She still loved the man even if she hated him for what he did.

Cliff nodded with a reluctant smile. "I mean, we would definitely have to leave for the time being. At some point, I imagine you will want to see your family again, and I'd like to keep some form of contact with Phyliss at least."

That was understandable and practical. This was why

they worked together. They just knew how the other operated and how to fine-tune situations between each other.

"I suppose I should start packing then. We can probably leave tonight. I've been staying with Bridget Dante in New York. At least semi; we can probably crash there. She is in Europe right now. I'm supposed to be joining her in London at the end of the month."

Something about Cliff's body language changed, "You want to leave tonight?"

"Why not? You can get the divorce over paperwork and proxy or whatever," Vivica explained. She realized his body language and eyes were quickly changing.

"You don't want to leave here tonight, do you?"

"Weston… It's not that I don't want to leave her. It's that I can't just leave in the middle of the night. I have to face her at least," Cliff tried to point out.

"Then tell her as you pack. You might get a punch in the face, but I know you can handle it." She almost felt bad saying that, but at this moment, she was very pissed off at him. He came here to beg for her to take him back and for them to run off.

Vivica looked at him straight in the eyes, "Did you come here to see if I would just drop everything to be with you again? Or did you genuinely want me back? Tell me the damn truth Cliff."

Where was the man who used to treat her like a princess?

Why had this man replaced the sweet boy that had once been the love of her life? Still was the love of her life.

"No... I do want you back. I do want to run off with you. I just..." Cliff explained. He just wanted to see if it was still an option. The sad thing was that it definitely was still an option, at least up until this very moment. It was time that Vivica moved on officially and forever.

"I'm going into the kitchen to make myself a drink. When I return, I want you gone. We will pretend this conversation never happened. You weren't here."

She got up and walked out. She didn't even look at the man that was the love of her life. It was becoming rather clear that he no longer existed for her.

This would probably be the hardest thing that she ever had to do. It was worth it. She wasn't doing it because she cared how it would affect her mother or sister. She was doing it because she wouldn't be the other woman for a man who should have made her the most important one in the first place.

Their life had been planned out since right before their senior year of high school. She and Cliff had plotted out everything while he was in college for the next five years. This wasn't supposed to be her life. This wasn't how any of this was supposed to go, and yet here they were. He was married to her *long-lost sister*, and she was single.

What would Vivica do next? She went over to the

kitchen phone and dialed a number. She was hoping that the right person picked up the phone.

"Hi. I'm so glad it was you who picked up. Meet me at the Harbor Inn. No, you know what? Let's meet somewhere to get drunk. Sounds perfect. See you there."

LANGLEY – JANUARY 2019

When she had originally lost her virginity, it had been a badge of honor amongst her friend group. Langley had made sure that everyone she knew was aware of it. There were many more conquests since that first time. Some amazing, some legendary, and some just downright weird. Yet, in taking Brad's virginity and finally getting to touch the man that she loved, it was just a different situation altogether. It was as if she had lost her virginity again. It was far from good sex. It was actually one of the most awkward feelings in the world to have been more aware of what was going on than Brad. However, it still was just perfection.

"So, how long before you and Brad are off the table? I just want to know so I can make my move," Amanda said as she walked up to her outside of Saint Agnes.

Langley rolled her eyes, "Why are you here right now? You aren't even enrolled yet."

Amanda laughed, "Always so wrong little Kingsley. I just enrolled today. I won't be starting until next week, though."

This made Langley's blood boil. Why on earth was Amanda Madwell going to school with her again? She wondered how much money Bridget had to donate on her behalf.

It was well known that Amanda was not exactly known for her sainthood. If anything, she was known for being rather slutty. Langley was, too, in Manhattan and Long Island, but not internationally, as she didn't have a sexual conquest in every state, nor did that appeal to her. Langley enjoyed sex because it was a pleasure. She wasn't sleeping around with everyone under the sun to piss off her parents or anyone around her. Yes, she had definitely slept with a few men to get back at other people. In her mind, this was rather normal. She just didn't think of sex as intimate. It was something that you did when you were bored and or horny.

"You do you, Madwell, and I'll do me just like back in Manhattan," Langley explained.

Amanda started to laugh again. "Kingsley," she whispered.

"You can tell people whatever you would like. You might have been queen bee at your prep school, but I was reigning queen of the damn city,"

which was why Langley made sure to remove her flat ass the first moment she could. That was the genesis of their rivalry.

Langley was a Kingsley.

Amanda was just the daughter of modeling agents. Big fucking deal. Both girls had whipped out their dicks for the sizing contest before. Langley damn well knew she won by a landslide. "Tell yourself whatever you need to, to get through your day. You had to travel far and wide to claim a name for yourself. I never had to leave the island that is Manhattan."

The Kingsley girl was about to say something else, but Brad walked over. He kissed her on the forehead. A public display of affection; that was a first for her boyfriend. "What are you two up to?" he asked. The innocence in Brad was so wildly different than what she was used to. It was a turn-on for her. She couldn't deny it.

"Just catching up," Langley stated.

"We were just reminding ourselves of a few things from the past." Amanda got up and walked away. She tossed her hair behind her.

The bitch, Langley thought to herself. "So, how is your day going?"

The Fitzpatrick boy took a deep breath. He looked at her, "Honestly? I'm better than I thought I would be." What the hell did he mean by that? "Not that I regret anything, I'm just shocked that I don't... that doesn't make any sense.

Langley sighed, "No, it makes sense. At least it makes sense in regard to you. I get it." She had no choice but to get it. The blonde girl had a feeling that keeping her blonde boyfriend calmed down would be a difficult situation in the interim of things. He was so used to being pure because that was what he thought kept him a good person. Now he had to find a new reason to hold on to that.

"The world is still spinning. The gates to hell didn't open up the moment our flesh touched. We will be fine. I mean, I am sure that we will be. I guess it's just weird," Brad admitted.

"Well, do you want to do it again?" She could tell he thought she meant here. Which honestly, now that the itch had been scratched, she needed to keep it going. "I mean in your room or mine. I don't care where."

Brad nodded, "Yeah. I mean not right away, but I definitely want to feel that pleasure again."

At least this was a steppingstone. It might not have been a big one for a normal couple, but for her and Brad, it was leaps and bounds. Things were going well for once for them. That is all Langley honestly cared about for the moment.

As the two teens continued to talk, but there might have been a third party with raven black hair listening in.

CLIFF – APRIL 1990

He knew he fucked up. Cliff wished that he could slap himself in the face for how he handled things with Vivica last night. Tiffany acted as if nothing had happened at dinner when he finally saw her this morning. She was at the hospital all night. Cliff could not figure Tiffany out to save his life. When he first met her, she reminded him so much of Vivica. Since Vivica was seldomly around at that point, it was partially why it was so easy for him to fall for her. Yet, he couldn't for the life of him figure out what happened from the time they met to the time that they got married. It was as if he had married a different woman entirely.

There was a knock at the door. "Come in," Cliff said. He was at the office today. He was always at the office. The door opened, and it was his father. The last person he wanted to see.

"When you are given a task, it needs to be done on time," Rodrick screamed at his son.

"What on earth are you talking about? I got my last sales report in well ahead of time," Cliff said as he stood up from his desk.

Rodrick rolled his eyes. "Boy, I'm not talking about work. I'm talking about your marriage. I told you to be good to that girl. She might be a Weston, but she isn't trash like the Whore."

There were times Cliff wanted to go off on his father. That was what his father expected, though, and Cliff just didn't have the damn time to deal with him anymore.

"I don't have a clue what you are talking about," Cliff explained.

He looked out the window and looked down on the streets of Detroit. Cliff could still see his father's expression in the reflection of the window. Rodrick had this all-knowing look about him.

"I happened to be at the club last night myself." Of course, he was. He had been a regular at that bar since he became legal. There was an old joke amongst the other members that when his father Benton died, he took over his stool. It was a sick joke to some degree. However, while Cliff had never met his own grandfather, he had heard many stories, none of which painted him in a positive light. Many of those stories were from his own grandmother.

"I happened to see you and Tiffany go into the dining room last night. Well, I also happened to see you leave early. She happened to come over and talk with me," his father proclaimed.

It was things like these that made him wonder how he fell for Tiffany in the first place.

There were no redeeming qualities of his father; absolutely none whatsoever. Yet, Tiffany spoke with him as if he was the true head of the family. His grandmother made it clear years ago that would never be the case. Vivica often spoke about her father and how he was a bit of a bohemian Hollywood lawyer. He wasn't exactly someone for cordial old-world rules. So, it made no sense that Tiffany would adapt those for herself. If anything, he always suspected that was why Vivica's mother, Gail, left her husband. Gail liked normality.

When he was growing up, going over to the Weston-Brash household had been like entering a TV sitcom. Gail worked as a secretary at Fitzpatrick Steel. DJ owned a contracting company that was separate from the Fitzpatrick family name. DJ honestly was the ideal father figure in his eye. Cliff took it almost as hard as Vivica when he had died. He had no choice but to stay strong, though, because Vivica needed him.

Cliff turned around. "Let me make it clear. My marriage, my relationships are not your business."

"Let me share some fatherly advice. I know there is a first for everything. If you want to take on a mistress, be coy about it. Tiffany will catch on, and if she is smart, which I suspect she is, she will just keep her mouth shut. If she isn't, then it's her move. She can leave, and you can make your mistress your number one. That all said, your mistress shouldn't be a redhaired Whore."

Cliff quickly picked up a book and threw it towards his father. Rodrick quickly walked out of the room, laughing.

Cliff knew damn well what he had to do. He just hoped it wasn't too late. He was going to leave Tiffany. He had no choice. This wasn't going to turn into a healthy relationship if it hadn't already. Which it really hadn't.

VIVICA – APRIL 1990

The red-haired vixen blinked. She then opened her eyes wide and looked around the room. Where the hell was she? The pastel-style room clearly indicated some sort of hotel. The last thing she remembered was meeting Nial at the Harbor Inn. No… wait, the last thing she remembered was Nial suggesting the go somewhere that served liquor. Wait, they were at the airport. Why did they go to the airport? Where was she? She turned to her left and noticed a naked blonde man sleeping next to her. Vivica quickly turned him to his side. Nial? Did she sleep with Nial? This wasn't really a big deal. Vivica could brush it off. They had both been drinking rather heavily.

"Nial." She said, pushing at him. "Wake up!"

The blonde man tossed and turned a bit. Then he yawned and opened his eyes, "Where the fuck am I?" He quickly looked up and saw Vivica. "Well, hello there?" he said kind of nervously.

"Did we sleep together?" Vivica asked.

Nial sat up in bed. "I think we did. I mean, I'm not wearing anything right now." Vivica looked around the room to see if there were any more clues. She then saw an open condom wrapper on the ground. It was clear that yes, they had indeed slept together. "Damn..." Nial said. He looked at her and changed his expression, "Do you feel ok?"

Vivica had no idea how she felt. She had no idea where she even was right now. "I suppose I'm fine. I don't remember anything. You seem not to either." She got out of bed. Luckily, she was actually wearing something. A shirt that she assumed was Nial's. Vivica looked out the window. "Are we in California or something?" Then she looked out into the distance. She turned around and went to the phone. Fuck, please have an American accent. Please have an American accent. She waited, and the front desk finally picked up. She quickly hung up, "How in the hell are we in Australia right now?"

Nial jumped out of bed completely naked. Vivica couldn't help but admire. He was really good-looking, "What the fuck?"

CLIFF – JANUARY 2019

"Are you sure we don't have anything to worry about when it comes to Nial?" Cliff asked his fiancé.

"Cliff, I have no idea. I already told you we will hire security. The only Fitzpatrick's that are invited are Brad and Perry, and Laura, if she magically makes an appearance," Vivica explained to him. She had insisted this over and over for the past day.

It really didn't shock Cliff that Nial magically appeared at the last minute. It was as if the world was cursing him for breaking things off with Vivica in the first place. This was a constant. When Cliff realized that he and Tiffany might not be compatible, enter Nial. When Cliff was finally ready to open himself up emotionally after Tiffany supposedly died, enter Nial.

When Tiffany returned, Cliff begged Vivica to give him a few weeks to work things out with Tiffany in the sense that he would make sure she was alright and then have her sign the divorce papers. Well, no, that didn't happen because, of course, enter Nial. Cliff was not going to let this happen again. Even Cliff knew that at the end of the day, Vivica deserved better than Cliff himself had given her. Nial was not the answer, not the first, second, or third time they had married one another. He knew that at the end of the day, at least in a minor way, Cliff himself was responsible for the supposed love story that was Nial and Vivica.

Vivica sat down next to Cliff on the couch at Northpointe.

"I have a few ideas up my sleeve that will fix things for the better. All you have to do is trust me."

He did trust her. He just didn't trust the people around her that usually were rallying things along.

"Vivica, just don't do anything that will get anyone arrested, sued, set on fire, or shot." Cliff often wondered if they lived a normal life ever. He knew that was a big no.

"I'm just glad that Brad is not as angry as I thought he would be," Vivica admitted.

"I think to some degree that has to do with Langley," Cliff reluctantly stated.

She turned to him and gave him a dirty look, "Lions heart, I'm not responsible for anything. She is just an annoyance that won't go away."

It often amused him how much Vivica put her resentment from treatment from others on to the Kingsley girl. They were more alike than different. Age was the only thing that separated the two women, in the same way it did with Vivica and Margot. Although Margot definitely was not a character who could be so easily dealt with.

MARGOT – JANUARY 2019

The CEO had to admit that putting Lucy in charge of the hotel definitely had its perks. She walked into Lucy's office and shut the door. "How on earth are you making this place profitable?"

Lucy was sitting at her desk eating soup, "I'm sorry, what?"

Margot crossed her arms, "This place is actually turning a profit. It usually sits in dust for the chain places."

"Oh, that.....well, I was able to get the hotel in the 2019 Places To Stay Guide on several websites. Plus, I've boosted our online presence overall. Many auto people who have business in Detroit desire an upscale experience without the urban setting. Obviously, Warren does have a monopoly of sorts on hotels, but well, you know, not exactly a luxury area," Lucy explained to her.

When Margot first met Lucy in Manhattan, she had this bubbly personality that was most definitely fake. It was clear she was playing the part of someone because that was what her employer expected out of her. Lucy was most definitely overworked and bitter. She suspected that her father and his dealings did not help either.

Lucy showed up sometime after in Grosse Pointe inquiring about a job. Margot could tell that she was still playing the same act. That's why she turned her down. The girl needed to finally lose her chill and become the woman that was sitting behind the desk before her. Unfortunately, that woman happened to be best friends with the Whore from Beverly Hills, but no one is perfect.

"This place is a rather small fry in comparison to some of the hotels you had worked at," Margot pointed out.

"That's true, but honestly, I enjoy the work so far. There is still a lot that needs to be done. We still need to replace out the linen and carpet in the rooms, which will probably only get done in early spring," Lucy admitted.

Margot laughed. This girl was confident. "I only invest in the profitable parts of my company. I usually let anything that slips up play out until they either fix themselves or go under. Then I sell what's left in scraps. I was not allowed to sell this place because of a sense of nostalgia that my foolish parents had for it. That said, how would you feel about expanding upon the hotel business further?" Margot had often considered investing in a hotel chain. She just never expected it would be this one.

Lucy looked puzzled, "You want me to be involved in a chain expansion?

"I want you to be in charge of the project, actually," Margot admitted. It was the perfect time for them to put forth the investment. "The only thing is that it will involve some traveling. I'd like to open up flagship locations. We'd obviously go about buying dying hotels throughout the country and the hot spots of the world; Toronto, London, Melbourne, Tokyo, to just name a few."

Hotels had always been a thing associated with men. Margot wanted to throw her name into the race.

The eldest Kingsley got up from her desk, "Well, I will have to think it over. I'm going to be honest, though, with Langley still in school; it is a bit difficult. Plus, Perry and I are still getting close."

Oh, this girl, she loved small-town life a little too much.

"You live in my uncle's old house?"

"I guess I do. I never really thought about it," Lucy told her.

"Darling, my uncle DJ, was a good man from what I remember, but his desires were a wife and child. Well, he could not have his own children, so he had to settle for adopting the Whore without adopting her. He never wanted for anything other than that. Do we know what happened to him?" Margot asked her.

"Well, he died if I remember correctly," Lucy said, confused.

Yes, he did. He died, and he died in his prime. Margot often thought of what could have been accomplished from her uncle had he lived; had he not gotten involved with the Weston trash.

"You need to think about yourself more. That sister of yours will be a senior in high school next year. Your brother is around in town. Also, Perry really isn't worth your time. Stay with him if you want, but he drags you down. Lord, how long has he been working on the Templeton Ice Cream takeover now?" She loved her son but really, "Just think about it. Don't think long, though."

VIVICA – APRIL 1990

They had finally found their clothes and found a spot on the beach to figure things out. Vivica was mortified. How the fuck did she get to Australia? What airline was foolish enough to let two plastered people on a plane?

"Hello? Bridget? Thank goodness I finally got ahold of you. Yes, I realize that it is late." She hadn't actually thought about that.

"Ok, look, I need you to get ahold of Myles. I might have done something really stupid. No, not like that... one time! Do we ever let things go? Regardless, I somehow ended up in Australia. I know I'm supposed to be traveling with you in three days. Well, I hit a bit of a bump, and now I'm in Australia. Ok, yes, I'll call back later." She hung up the phone and handed it back to beach boy.

Nial had rented them a cabana room. She turned to the Fitzpatrick son, her damn cousin, step-cousin. She needed to keep reminding herself of that. "Well, I mean, we can obviously get ourselves out of this easily. You have money, right?"

Her purse had mysteriously gone missing, so her credit cards were not of use. That was why she needed Bridget or Myles to wire her the money for the damn plane ticket. She knew she had the purse when they got to the hotel because the room was under her card.

"I mean, I have money to keep us going for a few days, to get back to the states, though. I'll have to call my parents or Margot," Nial admitted.

If he called Brandon and Nadia or Margot, then her mother would find out. If her mother found out, then she would get a damn Gail Brash-style lecture. Vivica, who was now a grown adult, sort of had no desire to listen to a lecture on getting plastered and ending up on a different continent.

"We will wait for Bridget to stop being hungover herself." What good was it to have a best friend who was also sleeping with the owner of their agency if she couldn't sober up long enough to get her out of this situation? "I'm sure we will be fine."

There was something off about Nial today. It was as if he seemed to be more or less into the idea of them being together in this moment. "We should get lunch or do some sightseeing. It will be fun," as he put his hand on her thigh.

This boy was clearly starting to have feelings for her.

This was not acceptable. Well, actually, she had feelings for him as well. "I have to warn you. Right before whatever the fuck happened last night happened, I had just had a very destructive conversation with Cliff. Nial, I'm still in love with him. However, I can't pretend that I'm not interested in seeing where things go with you."

"Why do you let that Knight control your emotions? Viv, let him go!" Nial looked a bit pissed off. She understood why completely.

It wasn't that easy to let go of a man who she had been in love with since she had laid eyes on him when she was twelve years old. "It's easier said than done."

"No. Give him up. He's turning out to be just as bad as the rest of his family always has been. You might not be a blood Fitzpatrick, but you come from working people who worked for everything they gained. Cliff Knight will never know that feeling," Nial explained to her.

She wasn't about to point out that he didn't exactly get into med school working three jobs. Vivica still understood where he was coming from. "I'm trying my hardest to get over him. I promise you that I am."

Nial covered her mouth and started to kiss her.

HARRY – JANUARY 2019

He was unsure of how to ask Langley about Brad. He didn't want her to blab something that she wasn't supposed to. However, the fact that Brad seemed both happier and more weirded out than usual was a concern.

The two friends sat in the dining room of Northpointe.

"Ok, what do you want to ask me, Harry?"

"How do you know I want to ask you something?" He crossed his arms, a bit offended.

Langley shot him one of her famous; I know everything glances. "Don't lie to me, Harry Knight. You want to know about Brad. I'm not saying anything."

"You want to tell me, though, don't you?" Harry could easily tell that Langley desperately wanted to scream something out loud.

She shrugged, "Well, I'm not saying that I do have something to say. I'm not saying I don't. I'm just saying that Brad and I are in a much better place. I also have been taking some very hot showers as of late."

What the hell did she mean by that? "Well, that's nice, I guess."

Seriously, hot showers? He knew that she had joked about taking cold showers because Brad had refused to sleep with her. He immediately turned all his focus on Langley, and she nodded yes. "You didn't? He didn't? He would never! Would he?"

"No idea what you are talking about, but yes," Langley said with the biggest smile on her face.

This was crazy. A few weeks ago, Brad said that he was probably not going to have sex until he was at least twenty-five. He didn't want to get married straight out of high school, killing Langley a little inside every time he would say such things.

"Ok, so then are we talking about this or not?"

The blonde teen started to shake a little bit in a giddy way. "You know I want to. It's like the only thing on my mind right now, Harry. It was good sex. Like was it the best sex I've ever had? Fuck no! It was good, though." She looked at him like she was in a state of ecstasy. It was sort of weird to hear her talk like this. "It's just the beginning, though. He wants to do it again. He isn't ashamed. Well, I mean he is, but he isn't."

"I don't know if I should be happy for you or concerned for Brad or what exactly." Usually, he would just smile and nod when Langley did something that wasn't exactly normal. Yet, this time a bit different. It involved Brad directly, and he couldn't talk with him about it. Harry realized that he was the one who had asked Langley for answers, though. So, it would have been a jerk move for him to change his mind on what he wanted the answer to be.

VIVICA – JANUARY 2019

The redhead sat in the lobby of Lucy's hotel. Things were on schedule. She sent Holly on a mission to find a pair of shoes at the mall in Troy, which meant she would be gone for a few hours. She sent her maid on the mission because she wanted some alone time with her childhood best friend, Brianna Belle.

Brianna Belle moved out to San Francisco after high school. They stayed in constant touch over the years but unfortunately from a distance. Brianna Belle, alongside Vivica and Cliff, were the three musketeers of Grosse Pointe back in the '80s.

It was funny to think that at one point, she thought that Brianna Belle had a crush on Cliff at the same time as Vivica. It turned out that Brianna Belle's crush had not been on Cliff but

Vivica herself, which she outgrew rather quickly. For whatever reason, Holly felt threatened by her childhood best friend, which was the exact reason Holly was in Troy right now.

Vivica put down her magazine, and her dear friend walked in from the front entrance. Vivica immediately jumped up and ran over to her, "It's been too long!"

"I know! We have to get together more often than when you have mental breakdowns and get married," Brianna said. To a normal person, her overly chipper attitude would come off as being sort of bitchy. Vivica knew otherwise. She was just that obnoxiously cheerful. As a teenager, it drove her nuts, too, after years of experiencing all the trauma in the world. She wished that the world could be like Brianna Belle.

"Cliff is at work. He will be joining us for dinner at the Harbor Inn tonight." She had no idea how she would keep Holly away from that. Maybe potentially remind her that she had a husband and children, but that might not get through to her.

"Oh gosh, I haven't been to the Harbor Inn in years. It's so weird to be back in Grosse Pointe. You visit me more often than I visit you. I really need to bring my children back here and show them where I grew up," Brianna Belle admitted.

Brianna Belle's family had not been very open-minded about their daughter being a lesbian, which was one of the reasons that she left town in the first place. The other reason was she was incredibly smart and got a scholarship to Stanford. She and Vivica really had nothing in common after a certain point, and yet when they were in the same room together, it was as if time had never moved.

As the two continued to reminisce, the lobby door opened, and in walked a familiar maid.

Vivica looked over. "Holly, what are you doing back so soon?"

"I found your shoes," Holly looked at Brianna Belle.

"Oh... you are here."

Brianna Belle got up and hugged Holly. "It's so nice to see you again! The last time I saw you was when Vivica was sleeping on my couch."

Holly shot Vivica a dirty look. "Yes, I remember. You are the childhood best friend. I'm the current best friend."

It really puzzled Vivica that Holly got so jealous of her friendship with someone else. It explained a lot, though, when she considered the fact that Holly had always been slightly cold towards Lucy. When the redhead first brought Lucy to her home office at the Fitzpatrick mansion, Holly had reacted rather poorly towards the situation.

The redhead adored her friendship with Holly O'Dell. It was, in many ways, the healthiest friendship she had ever had. Brianna Belle was a pushover that had been in love with her, and Vivica had resentment towards her because she had been friends with Cliff before she arrived in town. Bridget Madwell and her started out as friends after a disagreement, but Bridget often brought out the version of Vivica that upset those around her, mainly Cliff and her mother Gail when she was alive.

Lucy was a friend now, but that was after five years of resenting her for being a so-so boss, which is what Vivica was. She wasn't that bad. They got the job accomplished and got paid. There were only so many valid complaints. It's not her fault that people hired her for the spectacle of saying that she planned a party. The Whore from Beverly Hills.

No, Holly was different. Holly was along for the ride, money or not. She had no issue with putting her in her place, and it was something she needed. The only other person who really ever put her in her place in a loving way was Luke Knight. However, Luke and she were definitely not meant to be. Luke had made that clear, and she made that clear. It was a mutual agreement.

"So, then. I suppose I should point out that I'm the maid of honor. I realize you were the maid-of-honor at the last two attempted marriages." Holly said with her arms crossed. She looked like she was interrogating Brianna Belle.

"Oh, that is perfectly fine. I'm honestly just happy that it is finally underway. Cliff, I've known since Kindergarten, but from the time you two got together, I knew you were meant to be. I tolerated Tiffany because he said he loved her. I know he didn't. At least not in the way that he loves you, Vivica." Brianna Belle said to both of them.

It was nice of her to pretend that Cliff didn't have feelings about Tiffany. However, Vivica knew that Cliff probably would always have some form of feelings for his ex-wife deep down.

Unlike, Vivica who had no feels of love or romance left for Nial.

CLIFF – APRIL 1990

This wasn't going to be easy, but Cliff knew damn well what he had to do. He realized now more than ever that going to Vivica last night was a stupid thing without committing to leave Tiffany. He and Tiffany were just not two people who meshed well together. She had just happened to be there when he needed someone to talk with during a bad moment with Vivica.

He walked into their room at North Pointe. Tiffany was sitting on the bed reading a medical textbook of some sort. Cliff looked around the room. This was not his room. She had practically demanded that they move rooms once they were married as she wanted a view of the backyard and a slightly larger bathroom. On top of that, the room was almost pink. Tiffany had insisted that it was red, but even if the can said red on it, it showed up as pink. Cliff wasn't some overly masculine weirdo who couldn't handle the color, but pink for a grown couple's room?

"We need to talk," Cliff explained to his wife. Thinking the word wife was weird in this context.

Tiffany sat up in bed and looked over at him. "What's wrong?" she asked him. There was this almost fake tone to her voice. "Are you ok?"

Cliff sat on the edge of the bed. He looked forward instead of looking at her. "I'm ok. I mean... Tiffany, I don't think this is working anymore. I don't know if it ever did." He said it; Cliff finally said what had been on his mind.

His wife said nothing, at least not for a few minutes. Cliff finally turned around, and she had this look of disgust on her face. He thought she would be sad, but this look made sense, he guessed. "Are you kidding me right now? We are just fine Cliff!" She said it sounding both pissed off and overly chipper at the same time."

It sort of took him back a little that this was her reaction to this. "Unfortunately, Tiffany, I'm just not happy. I think we rushed into this."

"You might have rushed into it, but I sure as heck didn't. We said vows, Cliff. You don't just go back on vows," Tiffany explained to him.

She had every right to be upset. The issue that Cliff was facing was the fact that she did not sound sane in her tone. He was realizing now that he and Tiffany had never fought about anything. Either he gave in, or she just did, and he said nothing, a lot like the color of the walls in their room. He let her do it because he didn't want to argue. Cliff hadn't been together long enough with this woman for them to experience any normal relationship tropes.

Cliff turned to Tiffany once again as he stood up. "I'm going to go out. Obviously, we have to figure out the next step together, but Tiffany, I just don't think this is going to improve." He left before she could say anything. He expected to hear her scream.

Cliff didn't expect or really want her to come after him. He realized that he was coming off as a terrible jerk in this situation. It was something he would own up to. Which he was willing to. Now he had to go say sorry to Vivica and see if she was ready to leave.

VIVICA – APRIL 1990

"Ok… well, it would appear that Bridget is either still hungover or not taking my calls," Vivica admitted to Nial as she sat down next to him in the hotel lobby. It was becoming more and more obvious that they would have to call back home for some sort of help. "I mean, your parents will understand, right?"

Nial sort of tossed his shoulders back and forth, weighing in on the issue. "I mean, will they send us home? Yes. Will they go off on me for a month? Most definitely. The best way to go is through Margot."

The only way that would work is if they didn't say her name. "Let's just wait a little bit longer for Bridget to get back. It's not like I'm asking to borrow money. I just don't have access to my account cards right now."

She did have to wonder if her mother or anyone was worried about her. She hadn't seen Gail since yesterday morning, which could have been two days ago based on the time zones.

Vivica had to admit she was a bit confused. "Maybe I should call my mother?" It wasn't as if they spoke on the days when she was out of town. However, she at least let her know where she was. The last thing she needed was to be kidnapped again, and no one knows where she was. The summer of '88 was a weird one.

"I mean, sure you can." He reached into his pocket and took out some more change. Vivica stared at him while he did this. She couldn't help but notice the bulge that in his tight jeans. She remembered seeing him naked very briefly earlier in the day. Vivica assumed they had slept together the night before, and there was some regret in it. However, she wanted to have sex with him again and actually remember it.

"Here you go." He handed her the change. Nial had big hands. She liked them. She liked him a lot, if she were honest. This wasn't the kid that used to try and grope her when she would babysit him. He was a somewhat mature but not in a boring way, young man—a soon-to-be doctor, nonetheless.

Vivica got up and smiled. She sort of had a silent breathy laugh about her. "Thanks. I'll be back in a second." She walked over to the payphone and started to dial. Her mother better pick up the phone.

"Mother? Yes. Yes. No, I didn't mean just to disappear. No, this isn't a repeat of the summer of '88. I'd tell you if it was. Look, I'm stuck in Australia, and my bag is missing. I just need you to get my banking information to get a flight back to the US. Oh, I have done more bizarre things. Trust me, I have. I kept a cat under my bed for a year when I was eight, and you never found her mother. That's just wonderful... great, get my banking information so I can get the heck out of Australia!"

It had taken a good forty-five minutes of arguing with her mother to get the information, but she got it. Vivica and Nial had to wait it out one more evening together and would leave in the morning. They were left in their hotel room alone together. "I'm going to take a shower," Vivica told him.

Nial opened the mini-fridge. "Do you mind if I have a couple of drinks? I can spot you when we get back home."

Vivica shrugged. They could both afford it, "Sure, why not?"

HOLLY – JANUARY 2019

The O'Dell woman looked both ways before closing the kitchen door of Vivica's mansion. Vivica was supposedly going to a final cake testing with Cliff. This wedding was just days away, and now that the entire bridal party was together, it was time for them to discuss what they would be doing for the bachelorette party. Hannah, Lucy, Bridgette, and Brianna Belle all sat together at the kitchen table. Lucy looked overworked. Bridgette was texting with someone. Brianna Belle had a notepad that Holly wanted to throw on the floor, and Hannah was just sitting there.

"Hannah, what on earth is wrong?"

"I don't know. I just feel like I've been sort of absent as of late," she explained.

"Be happy you get a plotline at all," Holly said, sort of

offended. They needed to make this the most perfect day ever for Vivica. "Ok, hear me out, we take her to a casino. I feel like it would be a fun change of pace for her."

Bridgette looked up from her phone. "Darling, this is Vivica Weston we are talking about. We can't just go to Greek Town and lose a couple of thousand while we drink. We need to go big or go home. We want exposure."

The last thing that Vivica needed was any sort of exposure. "I think we need to think about the fact that this is Vivica's fourth wedding."

"Oh, well, actually, it is Vivica's seventh wedding. It will be her fifth legal marriage, though. Vivica and Cliff got to their wedding day the first time but never made it down the aisle. They also got married, but it wasn't legal. Then there was this brief relationship she had that ended in a Vegas wedding," Brianna Belle pointed out.

Lucy sighed, "Why don't we just rent a couple of rooms at my hotel and not do anything batshit crazy?"

Holly gave her a dirty look. "This is Vivica we are talking about. She doesn't do anything that isn't over the top. We have to think about what she would want."

These women clearly were not going to agree on anything. In her opinion, a casino was a great way to have a little fun without breaking the bank. Yes, Bridgette, Brianna Belle, and Vivica herself had fuck you money. However, Holly worked as a Maid. It wasn't as if she had a billion dollars saved up for a night out with the girls. Especially this group. If anything, they didn't need any of them for the bachelorette party. It should have just been the two of them.

"If we are going to gamble, then we might as well go to Vegas," Bridgette told them.

Holly thought for a moment, "I mean, I'm down for it."

Lucy looked freaked out. "I am not going to spend the evening rescuing Vivica from whatever craziness she can manage to get herself into in Vegas."

"If anyone would have to do that, then it would be me," Holly said as she crossed her arms. The fact that they hadn't had to rescue Vivica from her own head in the last six months was a shock to her on a daily basis. Holly was so used to her going through different periods of manic states that it wasn't even out of the ordinary when she would get calls from Vivica all over the world to go and pick her up. It was always an adventure in itself. The last time she was somewhere in Europe.

"We just all need to make a promise not to let her do anything stupid," which would be difficult.

"I just booked the tickets and the room!" Bridgette explained.

MARGOT – JANUARY 2019

Sitting in her library, she read the latest headlines. Margot put on classical music to drain out the screaming from upstairs. Nial was doing some sort of surgery on their house guest but didn't have anything to keep them calmed down. It was really sad that this was considered normal for her. However, it went past just Nial's antics.

Her damn parents had several hostages stay with them over the years, on top of the fact that she was married to a serial killer. Then, there was that time when some woman wanted to be Vivica and got her confused with Vivica, which was already a rather large insult. They both had red hair—different shades. Vivica was a crazed sex pot and dressed as such. Margot didn't look anything like her. Regardless, she started to hear footsteps coming towards the library and turned. It wasn't Nial, though, but Brad. "Have you come back for round two with your father? I can get you the code for the weapons safe if you want," she said half-joking. Margot wasn't sure for how much longer she could listen to the sounds upstairs.

"I've come to talk with you about the family," Brad said, as he sat down across from his aunt.

This intrigued her; she had to admit. "Well, what exactly do you want to know about the family? I mean, aside from the fact that it is a rather deranged family."

Brad rolled his eyes, "It just feels like we have never been able to move past our roots of being the poor family in town. I've tried for years not to be like my parents, but it doesn't work. You seem to be the exception to the family."

Flattery would get this boy everything in life. "I wouldn't say I'm any different than the rest of the Fitzpatrick clan. The only thing I do differently is to embrace the family business to the fullest extent," which was something neither of her parents did.

Brandon was always embarrassed by the fact that his father wouldn't give up on his dream of making it in America. Margot couldn't figure out why he would feel this way. The ridiculous adventures that her parents found themselves on had to be financed somehow, and those finances came from the Fitzpatrick fortune. Margot was the one to make them go from well off to rich. This was something that her parents frowned upon as well.

"I mean my father... he married his step-cousin. My brother and sister have just found themselves running for the hills to escape his antics," Brad pointed out.

"Well, they are also escaping your mother's antics as well. I won't defend my brother by any means, but at least he is the way he is, partially because your grandparents left me to raise him as a teenager. I didn't get the Fitzpatrick fortune growing up. I got my grandmother. Nial, on the other hand, did. Your brother and sister were not exactly saints themselves; I'll point out. However, they did grow up."

Margot had no idea what their names were. At least they seemed to be less stress-inducing than her own sons. Joshua Roe, the modern artist, and Perry Fields, the man in bed with the "big ice cream" herself Mrs. Templeton. Hell, if he was having an affair with Mrs. T, at least it would explain why it was taking so long for him to acquire her damn company officially. It didn't even make any sense as to why he would go after it. It was terrible ice cream.

Margot needed to accept that Perry was still learning his way. She needed to stop dwelling in general and get back to the issue at hand.

"The Fitzpatrick's are cursed. It's that simple," said Margot.

The noises from upstairs continued. "What on earth is going on up there?" Brad asked, a bit alarmed.

The aunt just shrugged at her nephew. "It involves the Costa family. Need I say more?"

"Aunt Margot, I doubt our family is cursed," Brad told

her.

She laughed, "Oh, darling, we have been cursed for years. Someone pissed off someone at some point before the Fitzpatrick's set foot on American soil. At least that is what grandma Ida used to ramble back in the day." She knew it sounded ridiculous because it more than likely was, but at the same time, it made way too much sense.

The Fitzpatrick family was dirt poor in Ireland and even poorer in America. Her grandfather Seamus was relentless in getting the Knight family to partner and fund him, which he could never do himself. It was her aunt Susan who finally got the ball rolling. Then, when they built their fortune, they moved into this house, where the last remaining prominent mob family, yet to move out of Grosse Pointe, just happens to live across the street from. Her parents took no issue with this, even if normal people would.

Then her parents chose to become quasi-professional spies, and things only got weirder from there. It also needed to be pointed out that her uncle died in a freak construction accident. He wasn't technically a Fitzpatrick or even a Bloom, for that matter, but he definitely counted.

She wasn't even going to try and factor in how Vivica did and didn't play some part in the curse and whether or not her relationships to the family put her in the curse or if she was a part of said curse.

"We are a very functioning but dysfunctional family," said Margot.

VIVICA – JANUARY 2019

"Ok, Holly, let's just be honest with one another. You are clearly taking me to some Bachelorette party," as she crossed her arms. They were currently at the airport at nine AM. The wedding was less than a few days away, and they packed luggage for a two-day trip, but no one would tell her where they were going. It was just her and Holly at the airport, but she had seen Hannah packing for something last night.

"I'm not going to confirm or deny that. I'm just going to say that I think you will be very happy with the end result," Holly explained.

It wasn't that she didn't want to celebrate with this group of women. That was in part why she picked all of them for her bridal party. That said, she would have been fine with

Greek Town. After years of partying, she had done it all.

There wasn't anything left to do aside from something so mundane that it turned out to be fun. She was in her forties. It was time to accept the fact that the days of jetting off to Europe or other parts of the world were over.

The two women got on the plane in first class. Vivica looked around and didn't see any of the other bridesmaids.

"Where are the rest of the girls?"

Holly looked around, "I'm not sure. They are supposed to be here, though." She seemed to be a bit taken back that they weren't here themselves.

The two of them waited a bit longer, but the plane started. Vivica looked at Holly, "They are coming on the same flight. Right?"

The maid looked at her phone. She realized it was in airplane mode. "Well, maybe they all overslept?"

All of a sudden, the captain spoke over the loudspeaker, *"Thank you for flying with us today. We hope you enjoy your one-way flight to Australia."*

It was that last word. Vivica wasn't even going to question how a plane somehow was going one way without a second flight. They were going to Australia.

"Oh no, this cannot be happening. I can't go to Australia. They hate me there!" She looked at Holly, and the rest of first-class all started to look at them.

"Can we get some of those overpriced bottles of liquor? I need to mix them with her Xanax," Holly said, looking at the nearest flight attendant.

Her wedding was days away, and she was on a plane to Australia. This was not going to end well. This was not going to be alright. Australia? "Oh lord, why did no one check our passports?"

"I suppose that is a good question," Holly said, a bit confused herself. "I'm sure we will be fine. It's been years since you have been here. We can just turn around right when we get there."

The red-haired vixen looked at her, "You want to spend two days sitting next to me on a damn plane? Me? A crazy white woman who freaks out over everything?"

Holly looked at the flight attendant again. "I'm going to need you to double that drink order! Does anyone have sleeping pills and noise-canceling headphones? I will pay top dollar. This bitch overpays me; I can afford it!"

The two women were in for a long and bumpy ride.

CLIFF – JANUARY 2019

Cliff was woken up early by Harry, Brad, and Preston to go for a round of golf at an indoor pavilion. Then, they went out on the Costa yacht. The only reason they didn't use their own yacht was that it was currently being waxed. It was also definitely not weather-appropriate for a yacht.

It didn't help when they found a chest filled with guns and white powder. Cliff chose to pretend that he didn't see anything, and they moved on to the next task. Laser tag. Cliff had not played laser tag in probably twenty years.

They were now having dinner at the Harbor Inn. It was a nice long day. Cliff realized now more than ever that he needed to find some adult friends. He had old-school friends that he would talk to on occasion. The issue was that he spent years being Tiffany's husband, and Tiffany had opinions on pretty much every person in town. They were only allowed to spend time with people that she deemed acceptable.

His former life with Tiffany had been a roller coaster. Cliff told himself over and over again that he had no regrets. He reminded himself as he looked at his son sitting across from him. He also remembered that he had Hannah and Hope. Those were things that Tiffany gave him. Vivica refined them, but Tiffany gave them to him. He supposed that he knew what he was getting with Tiffany. The same couldn't be said about Vivica. That happened to be one of the reasons that Cliff loved Vivica, though. She wasn't normal. She didn't try to be anything other than herself, which was a batshit crazy supermodel who loved with every fiber of her being and was a good mother at heart.

Tiffany was career-oriented and more interested in the idea of things like children. That was why Hope was unfortunate to have to admit her favorite child. She didn't need the extra attention that most people usually need. She was able to succeed without help. Hannah and Harry were different. They needed the attention, and Cliff hated that after Vivica left when Tiffany came back, he neglected them. Hannah wouldn't have run away after high school, and Harry wouldn't have gotten himself into the trouble he did had he paid more attention.

"Ok, so we will have a movie night after this!" Harry said.

He seemed to be genuinely excited. Cliff honestly felt like he was a teenager again. These were all things he would have done with Vivica and Brianna Belle or the guys on the basketball team.

"Sure, that sounds fine." He turned to Preston, "Is it alright for you to spend the night?"

Preston turned bright red as he looked at Harry. "Um... Yeah. I'll text them and let them know."

He didn't need Jackie Carson-Costa banging on his door at six AM, looking to blame Vivica for this if he invited him to stay the night. He wasn't stupid, though. They were all sleeping in the Drawing Room that night. He would make sure that Harry's bedroom was off-limits. "Brad, you could invite Langley if you wanted." Again, the upstairs would be off-limits.

Brad started to turn bright red himself, "I mean, I'll consider it. We should probably invite Amanda too in that case." Cliff nodded in agreement. His son and Preston, however, were giving Brad a look of shock.

Harry cleared his throat. "Brad, maybe Amanda has plans already."

"I doubt it. She's just at my mom's house all alone right now. Might as well extend the invitation out to her," Brad explained to Harry.

"Yeah... Great idea." Preston said, looking in the other direction.

Cliff looked at his phone. "I haven't heard from Vivica yet. I was sure I'd get a call or text by now."

HOLLY – JANUARY 2019

Someone needs to hijack this plane. Vivica somehow managed to take half a bottle of Xanax and down enough vodka and wine to make a fifth of something. Yet, instead of being in a coma state, she was still going at it.

"We need to get off this plane. Australia is cursed. Cursed, I tell you!" She took another swig. Holly had no idea where she had gotten that one. The flight attendant had cut her off hours ago.

"I'm sure we can get this all situated when we get off the plane," Holly explained. She still had no idea how they ended up on the wrong flight.

This was going about as on-brand for the two of them as possible. Holly wasn't even shocked they would get on the wrong plane and end up on the other side of the world. It definitely wasn't planned, but the universe clearly wasn't going to give them slack.

Vivica was about to marry the man of her dreams, and it had only taken her teenage years through most of her adult life to finally make this set-in-stone reality. This was the universe's way of saying we will let you have this but first...

Holly just wished for once that the universe would have let Vivica handle this on her own. They could have just gone to Greek Town.

NIAL – APRIL 1990

Vivica had been in the shower for a few minutes, and Nial had downed a couple of the bottles. He had to admit that there were thoughts racing through his head as well as below the belt. He was infatuated with her for so long, but now he was starting to have real feelings for this girl. She was a forbidden fantasy, though. Yet, they might have already slept together. They probably did. He couldn't remember, and she claimed that she didn't remember. He just hoped that he hadn't taken advantage of her.

However, if he remembers that she was the one who kept buying the drinks, why couldn't he remember how they ended up at the airport? That part was still a mystery. They must have drank the entire flight because they couldn't remember a single event past them waking up in this hotel room.

Nial had enough liquid courage in him, so got up from the bed and walked over to the bathroom door, and knocked.

"Hey, do you mind if I come in?" That was such a stupid thing to ask.

It took a minute, but Vivica finally responded, "Yeah, why don't you join me?" she said kind of awkwardly.

The blonde Fitzpatrick's heart started to race as he took off his shirt. He then slowly slid off his jeans and briefs. He was beyond hard right now, and there was no way he was going to be able to hide it. Nial walked into the hotel bathroom. The curtain was hiding Vivica's naked body, and he slowly slid it back to join her. Her body was perfect. He didn't want to be the first person to touch the other, though. Nial just felt weird, turned on but weird. All of a sudden, she started to kiss him. Her lips were so moist from the water and so plump in general. She grabbed his hand and put it on her breast. He started to caress his hand all over. He continued to kiss her but made his way down to her chest and continued downward.

VIVICA – JANUARY 2019

"How on earth was I supposed to know that there wouldn't be a direct flight back to the United States until tomorrow?" Holly said as the two walked into their shared hotel room.

Vivica looked around. This place looked familiar. "This used to be a different hotel."

Holly shrugged, "I'm sure that hotels change ownership here like they do in the US." She put her luggage down and sat on the bed.

"I know that, but I wouldn't have agreed to this place had I known that it was *this* place." She looked around the room, and it had changed. It wasn't the same room. No, it definitely wasn't because Nial and her had been on a different floor, but it was definitely the same shape and layout. Clearly, it had been updated for the better. "Nial and I stayed here on our honeymoon."

"I'm sorry, what? I thought you and Nial went to Brazil or something for your honeymoon," Holly pointed out.

Vivica sat down on the couch across from her. "No. That was the third marriage. I'm referring to the first one. When we accidentally eloped."

She still wasn't sure how on earth they were legally married. Well, they technically hadn't been. It was when they arrived back home that they made it legal in the states, but they had been married in Australia first.

"This is a bad omen, Holly!" said Vivica, who screamed loud enough people in New Zealand probably could hear.

The maid rubbed her forehead. "It's just for the night. We will be back on a plane in the morning."

The redhead stood up and looked out the window, "You realize by the time we get back, it will be the day of my wedding, right?" She was going to be rushing home to get married to Cliff. This was going to be a nightmare. "Holly, this is a sign. I'm clearly not supposed to get married to Cliff..."

Holly looked at her phone. "I'm going to go try making some calls and find us some food... I don't know," she stated as she quickly left the room. Vivica knew that was code, for she didn't know what to do next, which was not helping anything right now.

Vivica sat down on the bed and bashed her head against

a pillow. How could this be happening, she thought. "The universe doesn't want me with Cliff. I was never supposed to get with Cliff. My mother didn't want me with him. Obviously, that is the case right now."

She looked to the skies, "Ok, mother, you got your wish!" Suddenly, the blue velour curtains flung open, and a ray of light came into the room. "Oh, good lord, I'm finally dying."

"Not today," a familiar voice said. She entered from the bathroom; a woman who looked to be in her thirties walked over to her and sat on the bed. She had dark, almost brown, red hair—pail skin much like her own but blue eyes instead of green. The woman wore a white business suit. "Hello, Vivica."

Vivica quickly sat up in bed. "Mother? Mother! Mother!" She quickly wrapped her arms around Gail Weston – Brash. She had died around ten years ago.

"How is this even possible?" Vivica asked.

Gail broke the hug, "Sometimes, the universe likes to work in mysterious ways. This is one of those times. Now, what is this about you thinking I don't want you marrying Cliff Knight?"

"Mother, I'm not stupid. You never liked him with me. You insisted on him and Tiffany staying together," Vivica reminded her mother. This entire situation was surreal.

"Darling, I love both of my daughters equally, but at the same time, I raised you from birth and I was around you until the day I died. Tiffany was a different situation. When she moved to town, it wasn't as if we had ever been close. You insisted that it was over for you and Cliff, and I believed it. They announced their engagement, and I didn't see a reason to object," Gail explained. She had the same stern tone that she had always taken with Vivica. It still annoyed her after all this time.

The daughter knew that her mother was trying to use reason but felt that Gail should have grasped that it wasn't technically over for Cliff and Vivica. "Well, why did you think it was going to be any different than my other fights with Cliff?"

Her mother gave her a dirty look, "You left your wedding huffing and puffing and were missing for a month. Up until that point, you had never disappeared on anyone. I realize that is a different situation now."

That was a good point. Vivica had never run as far and wide as she did when she was upset with Cliff during their first attempt at a wedding. In her defense, she had no idea what she was doing back then and expected Cliff to go after her. This was something that he never seemed to do. It was as if he thought that she wanted space. Apparently, he wasn't a mind reader, which, deep down, she did know. "Ok, but then why did stop me from trying to get him back when they were married?"

"Vivica, you just answered your own question. Whether it made any sense or not, they were married. I didn't want to look like I was showing favoritism with the child I raised. I tried my hardest to stay out of it. I actually did attempt to reason with her right before they got married. Tiffany was insistent that they were in love. I wasn't about to question it. I will admit this once and only once, but you and Cliff were obviously meant to be together. You raised his children to the best of your ability even when you weren't with him. I don't think you would have done that had you not felt a connection to them, and that connection was not Tiffany." Her mother practically said this as one giant word. She said it, though.

It was funny; Vivica has spent years imagining a version of this conversation. It was finally happening, and yet there was something not satisfying about it. "Why do you have to make sense?"

"I'm your mother. It's always been my job," she crossed her arms and rolled her eyes.

"I suppose that's all you came here to do. To tell me that you approve of this marriage?" she asked her mother.

Gail nodded yes, "Unfortunately, that's all the time I've been granted. One day we will be reunited. I hope it isn't for a very long time, though."

"Come on, dear! You need to get back!" another familiar voice said. A head popped out from the bathroom door. It was her stepfather, DJ Brash. "Do us proud, Vivica, like you always do!"

Gail walked over to him and took his hand, "We love you always." All of a sudden, the curtains shut again, and the room went dark.

The door opened. Holly walked in and saw Vivica as she cried on the bed. "Oh, for goodness sake, I got us the earliest flight available. You will be back in Grosse Point with time to spare."

"Holly, I think I've had an awakening!" Vivica explained.

Holly nodded her head, "Ok, great, get some sleep. You've been drinking and popping pills for like twelve hours. Time to sober up!"

CLIFF – JANUARY 2019

After six or so movies, Cliff needed a break from the teenagers. He didn't really think he had to worry about the kids. The Knight CEO went upstairs to his home office but couldn't think. Cliff looked at a picture of Vivica on his desk, which happened to be one from their childhood. They were young and happy. They were happy right now. The memories they had banked over the years together were priceless, and he had to admit that even the not-so-great ones were at least tolerable because they had been together. Cliff loved Vivica with all his heart. He just wished that the people around him would have as well.

The door opened, and he assumed it would be Harry urging him to get back downstairs. Instead, he was a bit thrown back. "Hello, Cliff…"

"Grandma?" Cliff said in shock. It was Delia Knight, his late grandmother who had died over a decade earlier. She looked younger than when she had passed as if she repossessed her youth in the afterlife. "How on earth is this happening?"

Delia smiled at him as she closed the door behind her.

"I think the best way to look at this is that it is happening and not to question it," she explained to him. Cliff agreed that was probably for the best. "Well, what exactly brings you here?"

"You need to know that the family is behind you about this wedding. We are." Cliff was a bit thrown back on this. "Vivica was not my favorite person in life, but she was far from my least favorite person. I knew the love that she had for you. I was more than supportive of your first attempt at marriage."

The first wedding, Tiffany... His father... The world was against them back then. He had to admit that, at least to himself. "Well, why couldn't you have been more vocal about this in life?"

Delia shot him one of her classic looks. "Child, I gave you my peace of mind every chance I could. Tiffany might have given you children, but everything else was heartache." If Cliff honestly dug down deep enough, he had to admit that he did remember Delia being against the idea of his marriage to Tiffany. She kept insisting that Tiffany needed to be put in her place within the family. Cliff didn't understand that back then, but looking at the context, he did now. Tiffany had always been more obsessed with being a Knight than she had been about being married to Cliff.

"You never enjoyed being a Knight, did you?" Cliff asked.

His grandmother took a deep breath. "I enjoyed being a grandmother to you and Phyllis. I wasn't a good mother to either of my children. I should have been less hard on Clifton and harder on Rodrick. I should have left Benton years before he was shot. I should not have put up with Heathcliff's racism towards me. I should have never touched wine. A lot of things I suppose I should have done. A lot of wisdom I wish I had passed on to you and Phyllis in life." Delia looked human, which was a bizarre thing to think about a dead woman, but it was the best Cliff could come up with. His grandmother was the Knight Matriarch in an era where being a woman on top of being Latina didn't get her any points. This woman had raised him. It had never been his father Rodrick, and his mother was never given a chance because of Rodrick. The Knight household during his youth was a dreadful place. There was a reason why he had spent most of his time with Vivica and her family.

Cliff started to smile, "I'm going to marry the crazy redhead from Detroit..." His grandmother started to laugh alongside him.

CLIFF – SEPTEMBER 1979

Cliff had tried to dodge this girl all afternoon. She insisted on sitting with him and Brianna Belle during lunch. She wanted to be on their team during gym. It was bizarre. It wasn't that she was mean or weird; it was because she only wished to speak about Beverly Hills and how it was nothing like Grosse Pointe. Her father was an entertainment lawyer. Her mother insisted they move to Michigan. She just refused to stop talking.

Cliff finally made it up to his driveway and turned around. "So, I guess I will see you at school tomorrow," the twelve-year-old boy told the red-haired girl.

"Can I come in for a little bit?" Vivica asked him. The way she said it was as if she was going to do so regardless.

"I mean, yeah, sure," Cliff said, feeling a sense of defeat.

He got his key out of his pocket and opened the front door of North Pointe. He didn't like having people over because he never knew what was going to be going on in the house. He could hear screaming from the dining room.

"This is my home mother. You don't get to tell me what to do in my home!"

"I can do whatever I want. The home was willed to me. You might have the Knight blood, but I married a Knight man."

Cliff turned to Vivica, who seemed unamused by this. "Why don't we go into the Drawing Room?" he suggested. The two children did just that, and he closed the door behind them loud enough that he hoped his grandmother or father would take the hint that he was now home.

"I'm sure you want to get back home soon," said Cliff.

"I'm in no rush," Vivica said with a smile on her face. She sat very close to Cliff on the couch.

"I love how this is a rounded room. It's kind of like a castle," said Vivica.

He shrugged, "I mean, I guess. I never really thought of it like that."

The door opened, and his grandmother walked in. She looked a bit shocked to see the new girl with him.

"Hello, grandmother," he said as he turned back to look at her.

"Who is your friend?" Delia asked.

"I'm Vivica Weston!" she said as she jumped up.

Delia looked at her for a minute. "Weston? I've heard that name before somewhere. It's been a while. Do you come from out West?"

Vivica nodded, "Yes! I'm from Beverly Hills, born and raised until now. Beverly Hills is just the best place to live."

"Whereabouts in town do you live now?" Delia asked.

"Oh, well, um, towards the edge of town," she admitted. This came out sort of softly.

His grandmother turned to Cliff, and Cliff gave her a look of please rescue me. "Well, Vivica, I have to get Cliff to a dentist appointment. You are welcome back anytime." Cliff's eyes widened at this, "Just call first."

Vivica seemed to be a bit sad by this but grabbed her book bag. "Alright. I'll see you tomorrow at school then, Cliff!" She quickly gave him a hug which threw him by surprise. She then ran out of the room.

Delia put her hands on her hips. "Who is that crazy redhead from Detroit?"

CLIFF – JANUARY 2019

"It always takes men longer to realize that a woman has feelings for him," Delia explained. "I knew that girl was head over heels for you from the moment I met her."

Cliff looked back at his life with Vivica, and a giant smile formed. This girl had been a staple of his life since he was twelve years old. She was his Weston.

LANGLEY – JANUARY 2019

This wasn't the first bachelor party she had crashed. However, it was definitely the most boring. Harry was essentially hosting the sleepover that he sadly never got as a child. Or maybe he did. Langley wasn't exactly sure which version of events was less sad. He was her best friend, though, and she wasn't about to ruin his night. It was Brad or Cliff that invited her, though. Not the first time the groom had invited her to the bachelor party. The first time he wasn't trying to hit on her. Even she knew she would be in therapy at some point in her life.

Brad gave her puppy dog eyes as they sat on the floor of the Drawing Room. She wanted to sneak away with him, but they were given strict orders not to leave the room. This wouldn't normally stop her but considering that Vivica already hated her, she didn't need to cause any more issues.

She just got Brad to give in to her needs. The last thing she needed was to get banned from the house. "This is fun. Right?" Brad asked.

She wasn't sure if he was being serious or not. "Yeah. I love movies," Langley said, bored out of her mind.

"I do too," Amanda stated as she inched closer to Brad on the opposite side. Harry had mentioned that it was Brad's idea to invite the Madwell girl. Langley was unsure of the motivation behind it. Then she remembered that Brad was just way too trusting of people, including whores like Amanda Madwell.

Brad yawned, "I'm going to go use the restroom." He got up.

"Thanks for sharing," Langley said jokingly. She wondered if she should join him but knowing him, he actually had to use the restroom.

"So, am I actually welcome at this wedding?" she asked, as she turned to Harry and Preston.

Harry gave her a look of shock. "Why wouldn't you be invited? You are dating Brad, and your sister is in the wedding."

She wanted to give Harry a dirty look but stopped herself. "I'm just saying, your aunt doesn't exactly like me. I'm shocked that your father invited me here tonight."

"Oh, relax, Langley. If I'm invited, then you are too," Preston said jokingly.

That was a good point, the blonde girl thought to herself. She turned around and noticed that Amanda was missing. She turned back to the couple, "I'll be right back." Something was off, and she had a bad feeling. Harry and Preston were too comfortable being so close to one another, that they didn't even try and stop her.

The other day when Brad and she finally had sex, it was one of the best experiences of her life. The concept of virginity never meant anything to Langley. It meant everything to Brad, but regardless for her, that ship had sailed years ago. However, with Brad, it felt like a completely different experience altogether. It was almost as if they were experiencing something completely new together.

She continued down the hall at North Pointe, looking for the nearest bathroom. As she neared it, she started to hear noises. "No," she said out loud. There was giggling going on, and she recognized both voices. The old Langley would have burst in and slapped both of them. She wasn't the old Langley anymore. The blonde teen opened the door to find Amanda on top of a naked Brad. Brad quickly pushed Amanda off of him.

"Langley, I can explain. I swear it isn't what it looks like," Brad screamed. It might not have been anything on his end, but regardless it was something. Amanda kept an evil grin on her face.

There were a million things that Langley wanted to say. She wanted to scream, but instead, she just closed the door. Langley hoped that Brad didn't try and follow as there were no words left. She spent the last year trying to make this boy her own, and it finally happened, only for him to do this to her. He was no better than his own parents as much as he claimed otherwise. As she made her way out to the foyer of North Pointe, she heard Preston and Harry laughing together in the Drawing Room. Langley sighed. She walked out the front door. This town had both grown her as a person and stunted her at the same time. Enough was enough. She was Langley Kingsley. It was time to move on from all of this. The blonde teen got out her phone. "Hello, A-King?"

CLIFF – April 1990

"I'm telling you, Cliff, she hasn't been home in three days," Gail explained to him. There was just something off about this explanation.

Cliff sighed, "Mrs. Brash, I understand that you probably hate me, and I'm not expecting any forgiveness from you. All I'm saying is that I need you to let me speak with Vivica. I need to make things right with her."

Vivica's mother took a deep breath. "Cliff, if she were here, I would drag her out to speak with you myself. I might not agree with what you did, but I know that at the end of the day, you are Vivica's, true love. She is not here, though."

"Where is she then?" Cliff asked as he stomped his foot on the porch.

"Australia," Gail said, somewhat annoyed.

Australia? Why on earth would Vivica go to Australia? A car pulled up, and Cliff turned around. It was a black town car. Vivica got out, followed by Nial Fitzpatrick. What on earth was going on?

"Weston?"

"Cliff? What are you doing here?" asked Vivica. She looked a bit shocked to see him. She shouldn't have been shocked, though. He was here to make her dreams come true. Their dreams come true.

Nial walked up to Cliff. "You are going to have to leave. We have family business to discuss." He squared himself up to Cliff. Cliff admittedly knew that Nial was probably bound to win in a fight. It didn't mean that Cliff wasn't ready to throw a few punches if needed.

Gail rubbed her forehead. "What kind of family business?"

Nial looked at Vivica, and she smiled. She put out her ring finger. A giant diamond started to glimmer. It was gaudy.

"We got married in Australia!" Vivica explained.

"You have got to be kidding me." Gail and Cliff both said at the same time. Cliff walked up to Vivica. "Weston, I... I came here to tell you that I left Tiffany last night."

Vivica looked at him. Her smile dropped, "I'm sorry, Cliff, but I'm married now." She looked at Nial. She looked back at Cliff. "Cliff, I don't know what to tell you. I really don't. You told me a few days ago that you couldn't just leave Tiffany. So, go be with your wife."

There were many things that Cliff wanted to tell Vivica right now, but he stopped himself from doing so. She was right. He told her that he didn't want to just leave Tiffany high and dry. Yet now he had, and he had no idea what to do next.

VIVICA – January 2019

"I'm home!" Vivica screamed as she burst open the door at North Pointe. She fell to the ground and put her arms up in the air. Today was the day. The day she was going to finally marry Cliff Knight."

Holly walked up behind her with their luggage, "Ok, Lucy and the others are going to be here soon. Apparently, Hannah won at the slots, and then Bridget lost all the money. Oh, what fun we could have had."

The redhead stood up and looked at the maid, "I swear, there better not be any more surprises in store for anyone today!" As she was saying this, Brad walked down the foyer staircase. He was dressed for the wedding, but he also had a suitcase. She ran up to him and hugged him.

"Today is the day!" She looked at her son, but he was

not smiling. "What's wrong?" She looked around to make sure nothing out of the ordinary was about to pop out. Tiffany was more than likely still in Europe. Rodrick was most definitely dead. She had no idea where Luke Knight was but assumed that he would give them their space today. There shouldn't have been any other distractions.

"I'm ready for the wedding, and this is going to be an amazing day for you and Uncle Cliff. That said, mom, I'm going back to boarding school after we celebrate." He looked her in the eye. She could tell he was serious. Vivica looked at Holly, who just shrugged herself.

She didn't want him to leave her again. They were about to have the family they were supposed to have, which they had been thrown out of back in 2011. Vivica could sense something else was up, though.

"Are you sure we can't talk about this?" she asked as she once again looked at Holly. This time she was trying to tell her to get lost. Holly got the message and walked into the Drawing Room. Vivica sat on the steps of the staircase, and Brad followed.

"Why on earth would you want to leave when things are finally going right?"

Brad looked out into space. "I think in many ways this is for the best. Harry is my brother and always will be, and I've told him that he needs to visit even if it includes Preston as much as possible. I want you and Cliff to as well; Hannah if she wants. It's just best for me to be away right now."

"What about Langley?" Vivica said using the right name.

"Did that girl hurt you?" Her son looked away from her. Vivica could tell that whatever this was about involved Langley but also it was clearly not the girl's fault. Being his mother, she was not sure she wanted to ask what had happened. However, she would listen if he chose to tell her.

"It's just time to move on from this. I want us to have a great day or so, though. Then I've already made the arrangements. I'll be back at boarding school when you and Cliff go on your honeymoon," Brad explained.

She never wanted to lose her son the first time he went off to boarding school. It was neither of their choices back then, though. However, this time around, they were both very different people.

After all these years, Vivica was about to start a new life with the man of her dreams by her side. Brad had clearly lived a little bit outside of his bubble of sports and school. It was best that she allowed him to do what he thought was right as opposed to telling him no and making him resent her for whatever reason. "I love you, Brad, with all my heart. Now let's become Knights once and for all!" She hugged him, and he hugged back even tighter.

LUCY – JANUARY 2019

S he had no intention of enjoying herself while she was in Vegas. However, with Vivica not being an overdramatic mess, it made for a somewhat fun weekend with two women she hardly knew and Hannah.

She had to start getting ready but assumed that Langley would be hogging the bathroom. She knocked on her sister's door, but no one answered.

"Langley?" she said as she opened the door. There was no one there, and also, the room looked a bit like it had been semi-packed up in the middle of the night. There was, however, a letter on the dresser. Lucy walked over and opened it.

Dear Lucy,

I've left Grosse Pointe. I've known about A-King being

out of prison for a while. I'm not a mid-western princess. I'm a Manhattan queen, and the world was starting to catch up with me. I want you to know how grateful that I am for you taking Xander and I in last year. You tried your hardest to tame me, and in many ways, this choice comes from those teachings. I'm not running from you or Xander. I'm running from a version of myself that apparently is not allowed to exist. It will become obvious over time what I mean by that. You have been able to leave your Manhattan ways in New York. I let my guard down, though, and fell hard for someone thinking they would be different than the rest. They weren't. I love you. I will talk with you soon. I've told A-King to continue sending you money, at least through my graduation. You were an amazing sister and always have been an amazing mother figure to me. Enjoy the wedding today. Please don't try to rescue me from A-King or the city. I know what I'm doing, and this has to be the case.

Love always,

The Queen of Manhattan, L-King

The eldest Kingsley child sat on her sister's bed. She read over the letter several times. Someone had hurt Langley, and she was clearly running from it. She didn't think that A-King was a good coping mechanism, but at the same time, she knew that Langley needed normality restored, at least for now.

Lucy dried her tears and kissed the letter. Today was about the crazy redhead. Tomorrow could be about mourning Langley leaving town. This only made her choice easier, though, when it came to Margot's offer.

CLIFF- JANUARY 2019

Today was the beginning of the rest of his life. All he had to do was make it down the aisle in one piece. So far, all the blunders had proven to be temporary setbacks that both he and Vivica had been able to overcome. He got out of bed and walked into his bathroom. "This is it," he said as he turned on the shower. This was it.

"Hi, I'm Vivica Weston of the Beverly Hills Weston's! I'm sure you have heard of me!" his Weston told him.

"We are like the three musketeers always and forever!" said Brianna Belle. Vivica gave this dirty sort of a smile.

"Boy, you might not be a bastard, but you will always be a bastard," Rodrick told him on his thirteenth birthday in front of all his guests.

"*You will always be my Knight in shining armor, Clifton,*" Vivica told him at their senior prom.

"*How can you leave me for her? You rotten bastard!*" The love of his life screamed as she slapped him clear across the face.

"*Back off, Knight! Your precious Weston is my wife now. Viv, let's go.*" Nial ordered Vivica as they stormed off into the distance.

"*Cliff, we are going to have twins!*" Tiffany smiled as she hugged him tightly.

"*Of course, you are expecting twins... Why the fuck wouldn't you be?*" the redhead told her ex as she picked up her suitcase and scoffed.

"*I'm leaving Nial!*" Vivica declared.

"*His name is Harry. Harry Knight. My boy. My son,*" Cliff declared to a nurse.

"*Brad isn't dead. He has been living with Anthony Costa. Weston, Nial switched babies!*" Cliff yelled at Vivica.

"*Cliff... I tried to save her. I tried. She told me to save Hannah and Hope. I tried to run back for her, but the car exploded. Tiffany... Tiffany is dead!*" Vivica dropped to the floor and started to sob.

"*I'll always love you, Cliff, but I'm marrying Luke.*" The love of his life explained as she flaunted her ring.

"*I take thee Vivica to have and to hold in sickness and in health till death do us part,*" Cliff said on the day of his illegal wedding to Vivica.

"*Did you miss me, Cliff?*" Tiffany asked as she opened the Drawing Room doors.

"*I'm sorry Cliff but you need to be with Tiffany. The children need both their parents. Goodbye,*" his Weston said as she departed with Brad.

"*Nial and I have remarried again!*" Vivica said as a matter of fact.

"*I'm leaving Vivica,*" Nial said on stage at the Person of the Year ceremony.

"*Weston will you marry me?*" Cliff asked.

"*Cliff, I love you more than anything. You are my shining Knight and always will be. I've spent a lot of time thinking about what my answer to this question would be. So, my answer is not yet,*" Vivica explained.

"*I still want to marry you Cliff,*" Vivica told him as they danced together in the gym.

Cliff turned off the shower and picked up a towel, and started to dry off. The past was the past, and the future was only looking up. Cliff had his regrets, but from now on, all that mattered was getting married to the most amazing woman; a neurotic redhead who made him the happiest man in the entire world.

VIVICA – JANUARY 2019

Vivica sat on her bed in her mansion. She hadn't sat on it since she had been living at North Pointe. She still had no idea what she planned on doing with this. It was a house filled with so many wonderful memories and yet some not-so-great ones.

Holly was in charge of waiting for the dress to arrive. It was out getting steam cleaned one last time, and she was picking it up. The other girls were all getting ready. She had just gotten out of the shower and was prepping herself to do her hair and makeup.

There was a knock on the door. "Come in," she assumed it was Holly. Instead, it was Nial. Vivica quickly sat up. "What the hell are you doing here?" she barked at him.

Nial closed the door behind him, "Relax, Viv. I'm only

here for a minute. I just wanted to wish you well."

"Ok, what are you really here for?" Vivica demanded. She got right in his face.

Her ex-husband laughed, "Viv, don't act like I'm completely incapable of doing nice things." She gave him a nasty look, "We were married three times. Clearly, there was love somewhere."

"We were drunk in a foreign country the first time, the second time we were trying to inherit money, and the third time I was distraught over losing Cliff," she pointed out. It wasn't as if they had some fairytale adventure together. They had some decent memories but so many bad memories.

Nial sighed as he sat down on the bed, gesturing for her to sit down next to him. She reluctantly joined him. "You make me a better person, which is why we never worked out. I don't like being a good person."

"Are you drunk?" she asked. What the hell kind of a statement was that?

He laughed, "A little but even so... Vivica, you gave me two children. You helped raise and adopted my first son. You were just never in love with me."

She shot him a nasty look, "I was too in love with you."

"Vivica Weston-Fitzpatrick-Knight-Fitzpatrick-Fitzpatrick, you might have loved me at times but be honest with yourself. You have only ever been truly in love with one man. I might not understand it myself, but we both know that

THE YOUNGISH MARRIEDS | L A MICHAELS

Cliff is the love of your life. I was always a cheap knockoff," Nial told her.

That wasn't fair. She and Cliff had a history. At this point, though, so did her and Nial.

"When you wanted to be, you were a good husband and father; when you wanted to be."

He nodded, "Fair assessment."

"Why did you cheat on me the last time? Why leave me in such a public way?" Vivica asked him.

The doctor laughed, "I was tired of being good once again. Plus, the writing was on the wall. Neither of us was happy anymore. You were domesticated and had a party planning business. What the fuck were we thinking? You are a model. I don't like sharing, even if I share myself. Cliff has always wanted you to be you. Remember that I worked with Tiffany." He laughed, "She really is a bitch of a sister, as you have always put it. She was bossing Cliff around anytime he would come around. She wanted to be a Knight. As much as people like to call you a gold digger, you never married me for the name. You never went after Cliff for the name. Tiffany did, though, at least in part. She wanted to be a wife of a CEO. You wanted to be Cliff's wife. Obviously, things were not going to last much longer for the two of them, and I wanted to be me. I knew that if I escalated things far enough, Cliff would be Cliff and be your Knight in shining armor. Was I wrong?" he said as he looked at her.

Vivica remained silent for a moment. "Nial, I'm sorry,

but you aren't that smart."

He laughed again, "Oh, give me some credit. I know you well enough. I, unfortunately, know that car salesman too. I blame you for that."

There was always going to be resentment towards Nial, but she did love him. She probably never was in love with him.

"I tried to be in love with you."

Nial hugged her and smiled, "I know you did, but you deserve to be with the man with who you are in love with. You deserve to be with all of your children—Brad, Laura, Rod, Harry, Hannah, and even Hope. Which reminds me, Rod sends his love. Expect a gift in the mail."

"And Laura?" Vivica asked.

"Eventually, she will stop being the black sheep of the family. Until then, I don't think you should take it personally. She is our daughter. The fact that Brad has turned out so well is a shock," Nial pointed out.

She probably should mention that Brad was going back to boarding school, but she would deal with that later. It wasn't important right now. "Thank you, Nial. Now get the hell out of my room!"

"As you wish, don't worry. I have a final surgery today. I won't be anywhere near your wedding," Nial promised.

The door opened again, and it was Holly, "Oh, hell no! Don't worry. I'll go get the gun," she said.

Vivica jumped up from the bed, "No! Holly, we are good. He is leaving. I promise you don't have anything to worry about."

The maid gave Nial the evil eye, "I see you again today, I'm calling a hitman. You aren't the only one with connections."

Nial laughed and walked out. Holly turned back to Vivica, holding the garment bag. "Vivica... I have some bad news."

"What?" Vivica asked, confused.

Holly gulped as she unzipped the bag. Inside of the very thin bag was a knee-length dress that had was a floral printed dress.

"The dress you ordered was accidentally sent to someone in a different state. Don't ask how because, of course, they aren't giving details. This was the only dress they had in your exact measurements."

"I won't wear that. I will not wear a floral dress. We already ended up in Australia of all places. There is no way in hell I can wear a floral dress," Vivica screamed for a minute straight.

The door soon opened again. Lucy, Bridget, Hannah, and Brianna Belle all rushed in, "Vivica, what is wrong?" Brianna Belle asked.

"That dress!" she shrieked.

Bridget shivered, "Floral... not your style whatsoever."

Holly shot Bridget a dirty look.

"Australia, now this. The universe is trying to tell me something. It's trying to tell me that this wedding is not going to happen today."

Lucy yanked the dress out of Holly's hands, "Vivica Weston-Fitzpatrick-Knight-Fitzpatrick-Fitzpatrick. You are going to put this God-damned dress on, and you are going to get married today. I put up with Person of the Year ceremonies that we branded galas, and I put up with driving you around town because you can't figure out brakes to save your life, and I gave update nights to keep you from having nervous breakdowns at Mrs. Templeton's White Parties! White Parties! We might not have planned this damn party, but this won't be the damn event that goes wrong. I will get this dress on you and have you down that aisle if it means drugging you and doing a *Weekend at Bernie's* to get you married to Cliff Knight once and for all."

It finally happened. Vivica broke Lucy.

"Ok then, let's get me ready for today," Vivica said very quietly.

HARRY – JANUARY 2019

The curly-haired cousin looked Brad in the eye, "Why did you do this? How can you leave me?" There were tears in his eyes.

Brad could hardly look at him, "I'm sorry Harry. I fucked up so badly this time."

"You think? So, what is your answer going to be for leaving me? I have already lost my best friend because of you. My only friend, and now you are going to go back to boarding school?" Harry continued to scream at him. It was sort of shocking him that he was able to scream at his cousin of all people.

"I need to be away from my parents, my dad specifically. I can't turn out like him. I can't believe I did that to Langley. I don't deserve her forgiveness. I don't think she wants it. Have you heard from her at all?" Brad asked.

Langley left him a long letter. She would be texting him with her new number soon. She didn't want to talk until then. Langley Kingsley was his first real friend outside of his family ever. It was the first time that someone had taken an interest in him for him. She had helped him when he was still in the closet, and was there for him in the most bizarre way possible when he was outed. Now she was just gone, and he knew that she was not coming back. At least not right away. "She doesn't want to talk with you," Harry crossed his arms.

"All things considered; I don't blame her. I don't know why you are talking with me," Brad told him.

"You are still my family. I still love you. You fucked up badly, but that doesn't mean I don't love you, Brad."

He could tell this was only making Brad feel worse. He wasn't going to do that on purpose.

"Look, today is our parent's wedding. Let's get through the day. Am I mad at you? Yes. Will I forgive you eventually? Obviously, but let's get through the day," Harry explained to him.

He walked out of Brad's room and lightly slammed the door. In the hallway, Harry's heart started to race. He felt so bad about how he just left things. Yet, at the same time, he felt perfectly justified in how he handled things.

THE WEDDING – JANUARY 2019

It took nine years for Cliff Knight to realize he had a thing for Vivica Weston. It took twenty years for Vivica and Cliff to marry after a blundered proposal. It would take another eight years for Cliff and Vivica to make things legal finally. Today was the day that these two would finally wed.

Early on, they both realized that Saint Agnes would not allow them to marry inside the actual church, as Cliff and Tiffany had already been married there. Vivica somehow managed to get her third marriage to Nial in the church. This was fine for the couple, though, as they managed to secure the main hallway of the school. It was where they had first met. Sure, they could have married at North Pointe, but it wouldn't have been the same thing for them. The reception would be there, in the hallway, the place where Vivica followed Cliff home on her first day from school.

Lucy might not have planned the wedding, but she made it her mission to make sure that the hallway didn't resemble a hallway. On the off chance that The Fitzpatrick Group ever got back together to plan another party, she was not going to have a school hallway wedding be on Vivica's rap sheet. Lucy secretly hoped they would never reform the Fitzpatrick Group, though.

She could spot Perry sitting in on the Brides side, alongside Mrs. Templeton. Why on earth would Mrs. Templeton of all people want to go to the wedding of The Whore from Beverly Hills? She really didn't have anything else planned for the afternoon.

On the groom's side, you had a bunch of family friends, and a few business acquaintances. His sister Phyllis sat next to Sister Mary Newman. They were giggling as if no time had passed since they had last seen one another. Anthony Costa and his wife Jackie Carson-Costa sat impatiently alongside Preston on the groom's side. Preston seemed to be excited about the event, unlike his parents.

Brianna Belle had not been in Saint Agnes in many long years. It was surreal to be back for the wedding of her two best friends in the world. The memories they had shared together within this building were irreplaceable.

Cliff had been a close friend of hers for several years. They played basketball together. She had longed for a female friend, and finally, that day came. Vivica had been her first crush. She didn't know how to handle herself around Vivica for so many years, and Vivica was so clueless about the whole thing. She was honored to still be a part of both their lives after all this time.

Bridget Madwell sighed as she looked at her daughter Amanda talking with a bunch of her mutual model friends on Vivica's side. She loved her daughter very much. She just had no idea how to handle the girl. It was clear she couldn't leave her alone in Grosse Pointe. Bridget had to get back to work, though, as the Madwell Agency couldn't afford to have her away for long. Grosse Pointe had been a fond memory for Bridget once upon a time.

Hannah saw Xander smiling at her from his seat. She liked him a lot. He was a good enough guy. The more time she spent with Lucy, though; the conversations she had overheard Langley have with Brad and Harry, she wondered if Xander was actually Mr. Right for her. At the very least, he was Mr. Right now. Which she was honestly ok with.

The music started. Cliff took his spot in front, along with the priest and the bridesmaids. He wore a white tux. It was Vivica's idea that one of them wear white if she couldn't get away with it without someone making an off-color joke.

The front entrance of the Saint Agnes School opened. Holly and Harry walked in hand and hand. This was the most confident that Harry had ever looked. Preston turned pale from seeing how beautiful he looked; all dressed up.

Holly looked like she meant business. If anyone tried anything, she was not afraid to go to jail for her best friend in the world tonight. All of a sudden, the front door opened again.

Brad held it open, and Vivica walked in one step at a time. As much as she hated that dress, and she really hated that dress, she absolutely owned it with every fiber of her being. Her inner 90's runway model was kicking in at the right time.

Vivica made her way to the altar, and looked up at Cliff, and smiled. She couldn't help but smile. The couple then looked at their audience of guests. Three chairs in the front row remained empty—two on Vivica's side and one on Cliff's. Flowers were placed on each of them. For a moment, the couple, both individually and together, could see Delia, Gail, and DJ smiling as everyone sat down.

Everyone who needed to be there was there. Anyone who chose not to show up, such as Hope and Laura, would come around eventually. It was as if time halted around them. The hatred, the misery, the past, Mrs. Templeton, everything stopped so that Vivica and Cliff could finally have their day.

CLIFF – January 2019

"We are gathered here today to unite Clifton Knight the Second with Vivica Weston-Fitzpatrick-Knight-Fitzpatrick-Fitzpatrick," the priest explained, looking at Vivica as if there was more to this story that needed to be dissected. No one else batted an eye.

Cliff looked at Vivica. He had to admit that he had no idea why she was wearing a floral. She hated florals. However, she looked drop-dead beautiful. She was as beautiful as the day he met her and the day he fell in love with her. The day they finally married. The priest and everyone looked at him. He realized it was his time to give his vows. He looked Vivica in the eyes, "We were twelve years old. Sister Mary Newman was our teacher at the time. You wouldn't leave me the hell alone for a month. I had to have my grandmother pick me up from school to dodge you. It was because of Brianna Belle that I finally realized that you were actually ok. It was then the three of us became inseparable, and I think Brianna Belle can agree here." He looked over to her, and she was already sobbing herself. "It was written in the stars that we would be together. Fate just had a funny way of keeping us together all these years even when we were in our own private world apart." He looked to their guests at this point. Cliff knew that there were people here just for the spectacle of things, and he wanted them to know just as much as Vivica all the things that made her incredible. "You were the girl from Beverly Hills that became the princess of Grosse Pointe only to dethrone the queen and take the mantle yourself. You forged a modeling career first local, then national, then international. You became a mother to two beautiful children. That's not where you stopped with being a mother, though. You took in a child who had no relationship to you in Rod Fitzpatrick and adopted him to the point where he was your son and no one else's without diminishing the memory of his late mother. You took it upon yourself to raise my three children when I was not in a good place after your sister, who never treated you well, went missing. Vivica, I can say without hesitating that you are Hannah and Harry's mother." Hannah put her arm on Vivica's shoulder. Harry smiled himself. "You ran two successful businesses with no experience in either field when you went into them. You fell for me because of me. You can't even drive, so I know it wasn't for the car. Vivica Weston-Fitzpatrick-Knight-Fitzpatrick-Fitzpatrick, let's spend the rest of eternity together."

He wiped his eyes clean. Most men would wait until the last minute to write vows. Cliff had been rehearsing them and fine-tuning them for decades now. Cliff turned back to Vivica. It was her turn to speak.

VIVICA – JANUARY 2019

The redhead held back tears. It was hard not to start sobbing, though. She laughed in the pleasure of what was just said about her.

"Cliff, my Knight in shining armor… I moved to Grosse Pointe when I was twelve years old with my mother. I fought with her every step of the way up until I sat down next to you in class." She definitely could sense her mother's presence at this moment. "We got into so much trouble as kids, and it only got worse, but better at the same time as it went on. We had our ups and our downs. However, it took that time apart for us to realize that we were meant for one another. You are the love of my life; my one true pairing; the one person that I think of in the morning and the one person I think of at night."

She looked over to Brad, "Aside from my children, of

course," she laughed.

"You were the one who got me through DJ's passing. You were the one who got me through my mother's passing. You speak of me taking care of your children. I can tell you without a doubt that my love for them is as pure as my love for you. Hope, Hannah, and Harry have always been my children, even when I was far from them. I've been blessed to have them in my life in the same way I have had Rod, Laura, and Brad. The adventures that we had as a family briefly are some of my most fond memories. The memories we will have going forward will be even better. Especially with all the extensions to our family that we have now." She turned to Lucy and especially Holly.

"I know things now about myself that I didn't know as a teenager or in my twenties. I needed to become my own person to make sure that you and I could work as a couple. We are destiny. The innocent years have passed for us. We now know that we are living our lives somewhere between Heaven and Hell. I love you."

She took his hands. They looked into one another eyes with the same passion as the first time they kissed. The priest cleared his throat, "I now pronounce you man and wife."

Cliff went in to kiss her, but she beat him to the punch. She was no longer Vivica Weston-Fitzpatrick-Knight-Fitzpatrick-Fitzpatrick; she was Vivica Knight. She was Mrs. Clifton Knight. More importantly, though, she was Vivica. All the names attached to her over the years, including the Whore from Beverly Hills, no longer mattered. Beverly Hills didn't even matter anymore. She was right where she belonged.

"I can't believe I'm finally married to the man of my dreams!" she said as she turned to Holly at the reception being held at North Pointe.

Holly hugged her. "You've come a long way since we became friends."

She never really thought about it, but Holly was right. When she had met Holly as an adult, Vivica was an erratic mess. She was still an erratic mess. However, she was now more certain of the future more than ever before. "Here is to the future!" Cliff walked over and hugged her. "So, should we get going?" They were going to stay at a hotel downtown before going off to Paris for the week. Bridget had arranged for her to walk in a show. Cliff was insistent that she walk the show.

"Yes, but you should probably throw the bouquet before we leave." Cliff pointed out.

Vivica smiled. She walked over to the grand staircase.

"Ok, ladies, gather up!" Hannah, Bridget, Lucy, and Mrs. Templeton all gathered. Vivica turned around and threw the flowers over her shoulder. This would be the last time she would ever be doing this. She could hear a bit of fighting, Mostly from Mrs. Templeton. Vivica turned around. Lucy was holding the bouquet. Her former assistant and now dear friend turned pale white. Lucy looked at Perry, who gave her a look like this might be a sign. Vivica was happy for them.

Cliff walked over and took her hand. Their guests started to clap. Harry and Brad ran over to hug their parents. For the first time in years, things were finally perfect. Vivica and Cliff walked out the front door of North Pointe. She looked back for a moment. Detroit was far from the only city in Michigan. Grosse Pointe was one of them. A city filled with history. Doctors, lawyers, businesspeople, car moguls, mobsters, ice cream freaks, and models. Vivica winked as she said goodbye. Goodbye, for now, that was…

NADIA – OCTOBER 2023

There was something magical about Michigan in the Fall. The leaves changed colors, and the sun still shined brightly. The temperatures were cold but perfect against your skin. These were all the things that made Nadia Fitzpatrick confident in her decision. Several months earlier, after many meetings with doctors and lawyers and the bureau, Nadia finally decided that it was time. Her husband Brandon didn't even hesitate. He packed up their Florida estate as soon as possible and was ready.

The famed couple drove down the street looking on to Lake Saint Clair. It was truly a sight to see. "We will be at the mansion in a minute," Brandon explained to his wife.

They passed Saint Agnes on their pursuit. As they reached their street, Nadia took a deep breath, "Stop the car."

Brandon looked at his wife, confused, "What's wrong?"

"Mad scientists and crazy French Princesses I can handle. Grosse Pointe, on the other hand... just take a moment to gather your thoughts. This is going to be the last minute of peace we have for a while," Nadia explained to her loving husband.

The husband laughed at his wife as he started up the car again. They turned into the street. As they looked out onto the right, Anthony Costa and his wife Jackie Carson-Costa were going at it with Mrs. Templeton. They could see their son Preston and his boyfriend Harry laughing from the window.

The couple then turned to their right. The Fitzpatrick mansion. The first house they had ever lived together as a couple. The house was built with money that Brandon's father Seamus had acquired, thanks to Brandon's late older sister Susan tricking Benton Knight into giving him the money back in the '60s. They pulled up to the curb and parked their car. This was when the drama really started to unfold. Another car swerved into the driveway right past them. It was a Knight car. There was only one guess who would be recklessly driving a Knight car onto the Fitzpatrick estate.

Out popped a familiar redhead. Her friend and former maid Holly jumped out of the passenger seat and started to kiss the ground. Vivica Knight marched up to the front door and started to bang on it. Finally, Margot, Nadia, and Brandon's eldest child opened the door and walked out. She was clearly dressed for work. "I have a bone to pick with you, Fitzpatrick..."

"If it isn't the Whore from Beverly Hills... I've been

expecting you." Margot put her hands on her hips. Vivica smacked her across the face. Margot then hit her back.

The Costa couple and Mrs. Templeton stopped what they were doing to watch. Harry and Preston ran out and across the street. They clearly were unsure if they should stand back or break it up. Vivica tackled Margot to the ground. Margot, however, was able to get on top of Vivica. They managed to roll their way onto the grass. This went on for a good five minutes of back and forth.

Finally, another vaguely familiar face to Nadia and Brandon ran out of the house. It was Vivica's niece, Hannah Knight, "Aunt Vivica, stop!"

Nadia knew this was her cue. She got out of the passenger seat. Brandon did the same on the driver's side. Everyone stopped what they were doing. Margot got off of Vivica and quickly shot up from the ground.

"Father? Nadia? What are you doing here?" Margot demanded of her parents.

Nadia smiled at her eldest child. "I thought I would surprise you. I'm glad that Vivica is here as well to hear the announcement. Your father and I are moving back in permanently."

Why have Nadia and Brandon moved back to Grosse Pointe? Why is Vivica attacking Margot this time? Why was Hannah in the Fitzpatrick mansion? Is Holly really not working for Vivica anymore? Does Langley ever return to Grosse Pointe? What about Brad? Are Harry and Preston going strong? Will we ever see Hope Knight again? Or more from Xander Kingsley? What did Lucy decide to do with her career, and did it affect her and Perry's relationship? Are Laura and Rod Fitzpatrick ever going to actually appear? How on earth is Mrs. Templeton still alive? All these questions and more will be answered in the next exciting installment of Between Heaven and Hell.

Between Heaven and Hell will return!

ACKNOWLEDGEMENTS

The "Cliffica" trilogy is over. Does that mean Between Heaven and Hell is over? Hell no! Between Heaven and Hell started out its life as a two-page story bible for an intended web series entitled "Grosse Pointe: The Series" in which it stared Carla, Dalton, and Lorelei Kingsley. It sort of just stayed in limbo for a number of years. In 2015, the name Vivica Fitzgerald popped into my head. I edited this to Vivica Fitzpatrick after a while. It once again ended up sitting nowhere. Then I was working on my passion project and coming up with a future plot line for one of the characters. He was going to write for a soap opera. I became invested in writing what the plot of this show would be about. "The Turning Tides" which incorporated the Vivica character with the Kingsley characters of Grosse Pointe. It's now 2017. I'm tired of sitting around with a trunked book that I have eighty drafts of in one form or another. I decide I need to write another book before I can focus on publishing that book. I turn to "The Turning Tides" but I don't like the title anymore. I write character bios for over sixty something characters stemming from the 1960's going decade by decade into the 2010's. There are two constants. The Knight and Fitzpatrick families. I introduce a different core family that fades out with each decade as they either blend into one of the families or go into obscurity. The late 70's saw Gail and Vivica Weston. The 2000's saw the O'Dell family with their daughter Holly. The 2010's saw an assistant moving to town named Lucy Kingsley.

The Costa's are an obvious homage to a popular daytime super couple. However, are even more so a nod and thank you to the late great Jackie Collins and her mob related stories of "Lucky Santangelo." The core families all go to the same private school. Saint Agnes. A nod to the late great Agnes Nixon. The creator of "All My Children" and the show that changed my life "One Life to Live." Between Heaven and Hell was the working title for "One Life to Live." It was too scandalous in 1968. It's not scandalous enough for 2018 when the first novel is set. The Knight family live off Bell Street. Named for Bill Bell Senior. The creator "The Bold and the Beautiful" and "The Young and the Restless" as well as co-creator of "Another World" and "Our Private World Apart" as well as being the man who saved "Days of Our Lives from cancelation. The Fitzpatrick family live on Phillips Street. Irna Phillips created the whole genre. "Guiding Light" and "As the World Turns" being her creations. I thank Ms. Collins, Mrs. Nixon, Mr. Bell, and Ms. Phillips for their inspirations. I never met them but they inspired me greatly and continue to do so...

I would like to thank Luviiilove my artist from the bottom of my heart. You brought Vivica and Langley to life. You made these two characters that I literally dreamt of a more real experience. One has to realize that I give Luvi a muse to work off of with an outfit. They go above and beyond to make these characters look alike. "Young Cliff" and "Young Vivica" as we refer to them are different character models. Yet, they manage to make them look as if they are the same person. It's on top of this that they were able to change the normal style that Luvi does with a more "romance" style for my stand alone "I Love You, I Hate You, I Miss You." Our longtime collaboration is far from over. If anything, it's just about to get even more exciting and ambitious.

Josh Patterson... You've supported me from the beginning of this bizarre journey. I don't think you understand the amount of gratitude I have towards you in general. I don't understand how it has taken you four years to read a book... That doesn't matter. You have been there. You have been the exception to a lot of people that have come and gone. Thank you.

Nikki Baker, we started out as two people obsessed with musical theatre. You were an extra on that one network show about singing in high school. We spent a Christmas half-cross country DM'ing while I re-watched "Daria" for the first time in more than a decade. We've gone on bizarre business ventures together that most people wouldn't have dared to go on. 2021 is the year we start the next business venture and the world is only just starting to know it.

Mercy Rogers, you much like Josh have been an exception to the people that have come and gone in my life. We've moved kitchen equipment together, catered, got lost on the way to see a musical, and saw a drag show together. You were a regular customer who went through my checkout line at grocery store. You are now my family.

It was 2008... We had gotten "Soap net" from our cable provider because I wanted to see this show that wasn't even a soap opera. You were watching an episode of "General Hospital" explaining how Sarah Joy Brown was playing Claudia but used to play the role of Carly that Laura Wright was playing. You were heartbroken when "All My Children" and "One Life to Live" went off the air. I wrote a years' worth of fan fiction to tell you what happened next in Pine Valley and Llanview. You once lamented how Erica Kane went through the same trials and tribulations as yourself. I'm not sure how accurate that examination was but regardless... It's because of you Lisa Marie Lobaito that I am where I am at as of current. This book would not exist without you slipping on your soaps during the days enough for me to keep curiosity going into my head on why these things exist. I love you. I miss you every day.

My Editors throughout this series... Sandra Watts and Sadie Faith Anderson. Thank you for making my words better and by that making the story in my mind flow on paper. My now permanent book formatter (so long as I'm the one publishing at least) Polyarts36. You do a lot without complaints. You more than exceed expectations. My video person vWebs123 you also go above and beyond expectations and do it in a very quick turnaround as well.

Ryan Welsh you've been a great friend and have shared my advertisements when I've asked. Thank you. Carol Roth... I know how I came to know you but I'm shocked and in awe that you acknowledge my existence on a regular basis. Thank you for sharing "The Innocent Years" and "I Love You, I Hate You, I Miss You" with your audience. There is no doubt that there are people in your social media audience that own a lighthearted romance and queer slice of life novel that probably wouldn't otherwise. Thank you as well for buying a copy of "The Innocent Years." Miss Buff Faye aka Shayne Windmeyer, you are my queen! Thank you for your support and kindness. For my brother Alexander who helped me attempt formatting the first novel, thank you.

Finally, the people who buy my books. Whether you like them or not. Thank you for supporting me on this journey. It's not over by any stretch of the means. Between Heaven and Hell is not over. It's just going in two different directions. Which will only become clearer as time goes on. On top of that expect titles that are independent of that universe and maybe even a little magical.

ABOUT THE AUTHOR

L A Michaels was born in Troy, Michigan and raised in Lake Orion, Michigan. L A has also lived in Wichita Kansas and Rock Hill, South Carolina over a two-year period. Currently, L A lives in Warren, Michigan.

A major fan of Soap Operas, L A grew up watching the *ABC* daytime lineup with his late mother, while discovering shows like *Guiding Light*, *As the World Turns*, *The Bold and the Beautiful*, *The Young and the Restless*, *Days of Our Lives*, and *Dynasty* on his own. Comic books, world history, drag, and theatre have also played a large part in his life.

FOLLOW L A ON:

TWITTER: @LAMICHAELS1995

INSTAGRAM: @LAMICHAELSAUTHOR

FACEBOOK: L A MICHAELS

FOLLOW LUVIIILOVE THE COVER ARTIST ON DEVIANT ART

www.ingramcontent.com/pod-product-compliance
Lightning Source LLC
Chambersburg PA
CBHW011130100726
47898CB00009B/2927